To Roby

Best for a terrific future

John Scully

A COMEDY OF TERROR

John Scully

A Comedy of Terror

ISBN: 978-1-990589-03-4
MacKenzie Publishing
Halifax, Nova Scotia
March 2022

Back cover photo: Emma Scully

Editor: C.A. MacKenzie
(writingwicket@gmail.com)

Cover Design: SelfPubBookCovers.com/Daniela

Canadian spelling is used throughout.

MacKenzie Publishing

DISCLAIMER

This book is a fictional dramatization, sometimes based on real events drawn from the author's personal experiences.

For dramatic and narrative purposes, the book contains fictionalized scenes, composite and representative characters and dialogue, and time compression.

Though public figures are named, the scenes and dialogue are the author's creation. The views, opinions, and dialogue expressed in the book are those of the characters only and do not necessarily reflect or represent the views and opinions held by the individuals on which those characters are based. Content provided by the author is not intended to malign any religion, ethnic group, club, organization, company, individual, or anyone or anything.

Views and opinions expressed by the author (where opinions are expressed) are those of the author and do not necessarily reflect the opinion of the publisher.

Neither the author nor the publisher will be held liable or responsible for any actual or perceived loss or damage to any person or entity, caused or alleged to have been caused, directly or indirectly, by anything in this book. If you do not accept this, please do not continue.

For

Toni, Jerome, Emma, Liam, and Eva

A COMEDY OF TERROR

CONTENTS

CAST OF MAIN CHARACTERS

Fiction Characters

Ayub el-Sahafat, Chief Petty Officer, Libyan

Bill Playter, Chief Superintendent MI6

Billy McFadden (Major William McFadden), Special Air Services, Parachute Regiment

Bob Cartwright, CIA agent

John McGuigan, Commander in Chief of the Belfast Brigade, Provisional Irish Republican Army

Malcolm Forbes-Smythe, head of MI6

Mariam Hussein, wife of Yuseff Hussein

Mustaffa Fakih, senior London correspondent for the Egyptian newspaper *Al-Ahram*

Teddy Williamson, Chief Superintendent MI6 (successor to Bill Playter)

Tommy Beecham, Malcolm Forbes-Smythe's private secretary

Yuseff Hussein, chauffeur, Algerian

Non-Fiction Characters

Abdul Qadeer Khan (A.K.) (April 1936-October 10, 2021), Muslim, Pakistani physicist, employed by Urenco, a consortium making nuclear equipment

Indira Priyadarshini Gandhi (November 19, 1917-October 31, 1984), 3rd Prime Minister of India from January 1966 to March 1977 and again from January 1980 until assassination in October 1984

Jack McCabe (1916-December 30, 1971), master bomb maker, Quartermaster General of the Provisional Irish Republican Army from 1969-1971

James Rodney Schlesinger (February 15, 1929- March 27, 2014), Secretary of Defense from 1973 to 1975, America's first Secretary of Energy from 1977 to 1979

Joe Cahill (May 19, 1920-July 23, 2004), Chief of Staff of the Provisional Irish Republican Army (key figure in its founding)

Muammar Muhammad Abu Minyar al-Gaddafi (c. 1942-October 20, 2011), Libyan revolutionary, politician, and political theorist

Osama bin Mohammed bin Awad bin Laden (March 10, 1957-May 2, 2011), Saudi terrorist and founder of the Pan-Islamic militant organization al-Qaeda

Queen Elizabeth II (Elizabeth Alexandra Mary Windsor) (21 April 1926-), Queen of the United Kingdom and 14 other Commonwealth realms

Sayyid Ruhollah Musavi Khomeini (September 24, 1902-June 3, 1989), also known as Ayatollah Khomeini, Iranian political and religious leader who served as the 1st Supreme Leader of Iran from 1979 until his death in 1989

Zulfikar Ali Bhutto (January 5, 1928-April 4, 1979), Pakistani barrister and politician, 4th President of Pakistan from 1971 to 1973, 9th Prime Minister from 1973 to 1977

United Kingdom Prime Ministers:

> **James Harold Wilson** (March 11, 1916-May 24, 1995), Prime Minister from October 1964 to June 1970, and again from March 1974 to April 1976
>
> **Sir John Major** (March 29, 1943-), Prime Minister from 1990 to 1997

United States Presidents:

> **Richard Milhouse Nixon** (January 9, 1913-April 22, 1994), 37th President of the United States from 1969 to 1974
>
> **James (Jimmy) Earl Carter, Jr.** (October 1, 1924-) 39th President of the United States from 1977 to 1981
>
> **Ronald Wilson Reagan** (February 6, 1911-June 5, 2004), 40th President of the United States from 1981 to 1989

United States Secretaries of State:

> **Henry Alfred Kissinger** (September 22, 1973-January 20, 1977), 56th Secretary of State from January 20, 1969-November 3, 1975
>
> **Cyrus Roberts Vance, Sr.** (March 27, 1917-January 12, 2002), 57th Secretary of State from 1977 to 1980
>
> **Alexander (Al) Meigs Haig, Jr.** (December 2, 1924-February 20, 2010), 59th Secretary of State from January 22, 1981-July 5, 1982

CHAPTER ONE

March 27, 1973

"I told them not to come into the port. I ordered them to stay in international waters. What the hell are they doing?" Chief Petty Officer Ayub el-Sahafat, the Libyan in charge of four of his top supply officers, creased his brow and peered out towards the three-mile limit. The boat was heading straight towards him.

"Should we blow it out of the water?" another officer asked, already picking up the phone.

"No. No. That would attract too much attention. Why doesn't their radio work? I thought we were dealing with professionals."

"They had their orders. Wait in international waters. As soon as it gets dark, give us a signal and we'll bring the consignment out to them. Couldn't be much simpler."

The consignment weighed five tons and consisted of 250 AK-47 and ArmaLite rifles, 250 pistols, twenty thousand rounds of ammunition, enough of the distinctive orange-red Czech plastic explosive Semtex to blow half a city apart, plus a black attaché case weighted down in case it had to be ditched.

The Colonel, Muammar Muhammad Abu Minyar al-Gaddafi, had approved the operation. He had personally met with the men who wanted the weapons, and he gave them away, free of charge. He also gave them a surprise bonus.

Gaddafi knew a lot about the Irish situation and even chided his guests for speaking English, not Gaelic. But *they* would have to figure out how to get the armaments back home without drawing attention to Libya. That meant total secrecy at home. No one but Gaddafi and his tiny cabal could know.

On board the small cargo ship, the German captain and his three passengers were frantic.

"Jeezus," Joe Cahill said. "They'll kill us. They said do not go into Tripoli. The port is watched all the time. By them and by the fucking satellites. A broken radio. Unbelievable. We almost lose a revolution because of a broken radio. Still, we don't have a choice. Keep going in, captain."

"Are you sure, Joe?"

"No, I'm not bloody sure, but if we don't, the whole operation is dead and we lose our connection with Gaddafi. We've got to risk it. In we go, my old son, and I'll see if my famous Irish bullshit will get us out of this one."

Joe Cahill, the chief of staff of the Provisional Irish Republican Army, Belfast Brigade, was not quite as cocky as he sounded. Joe was fifty-three, short, balding, and just beginning to form a cough. He had worked for a couple of years at the Harland & Wolff shipyards in Belfast, Northern Ireland, when he wasn't fighting or in jail. A cough, not a gun, would eventually kill him. The shipyards had given him terminal asbestosis.

He was born in Belfast amid the violence of the Irish uprising in 1920, just a petrol-bomb's throw from the home of James Connolly, one of the Republican Movement's leaders, who was executed by the British for his role in the abortive Easter 1916 uprising. Joe had joined the IRA as an eighteen-year-old. For the rest of his life, he fought to drive the British out of the north. He had been sentenced to death for the murder of a police officer but was eventually released from prison after political pressure from Dublin and, some say, the Vatican.

Joe was a Marxist revolutionary with every drop of his blood, and Gaddafi would negotiate only with the veteran boss. But was Joe losing his edge? How had he fucked up with the radio? A freedom fighter who loses his edge is a dead terrorist; he knew that.

He glanced across at his quartermaster-general, Jack McCabe, an IRA veteran and master bomb maker. In a few weeks, Jack would be the one to lose his edge. He would break one of his own cardinal rules: do not mix bomb material with anything metal. He'd get lazy and pull a shovel from the garage wall. As concrete and metal collided, a spark would ignite the explosives and blow Jack into the next world before he could say, "I knew I shouldn't have done that."

On shore, the Libyans decided to give their clients hell for breaking the rules, but they conceded a broken radio probably wasn't anybody's fault. They would load the ship as quickly as they could and disappear into the heat of the night.

By now, the lead officer could read the name of the small unremarkable cargo ship: *Claudia*. No doubt what the IRA had wanted—nothing to stand out. But the Libyans had been more careful than the IRA, who had acquired the *Claudia* through a European intermediary. Libyan intelligence had checked out the vessel and found it was known as a gunrunner. They didn't tell the IRA, but they had cut the load from the agreed forty tons of weaponry to merely five so the ship would not look too heavy in the water.

The *Claudia* pulled alongside the Tripoli dock, and without much conversation, loading began. Joe did have a few words with Ayub, the Libyan chief petty officer, who told him not to let it happen again.

"Don't argue about not all the weapons being there," Ayub said, "and please get out of here before anyone sees what is going on, especially the Secret Police."

Joe didn't know it either, but Ayub was also losing his edge, and in a few days, perhaps a lot more, he'd pay for his carelessness this night. But Ayub was a supremely confident officer, especially since Gaddafi had given him a much more interesting assignment.

"My friends in Pakistan want something very special from us. I said yes. They will pay. But it cannot be traced back to us," Gaddafi had said.

"What do they want?" Ayub asked.

Gaddafi had looked hard at Ayub, the younger officer, in full naval whites.

Ayub was a mere five feet five inches, with a razor-like brain. He was a Bedouin who spoke fluent English. He had mastered the language while training at the Royal Navy's historic sprawling base in Portsmouth, England. Not only had Ayub improved his English, but he had also mastered the intricate art of reading operations manuals, courtesy of an arrangement with weapons makers, such as Hawker Siddeley. Libya was still—sort of—on the Brits' good side.

Gaddafi, also a Bedouin, was born in the desert in 1942. The Colonel ruled as many Bedouins do: through trust, instinct, loyalty, and extreme calculating smarts. If you crossed him, you died.

"Pakistan wants an atomic bomb," Gaddafi had said. "And so do I. Get it for me."

"British Airways. How may I help you?"

"I'd like to book two return seats to Tripoli, Libya, please," the quiet but assertive British government spy requested.

"Certainly, sir. Now, tell me, when do you want to fly and your cities of destination?"

"We'd like to leave London on April the second, fly to Tripoli, and return to Shannon in Ireland, on—well, can I leave that sector open?"

"Yes, of course. But you'll have to change planes in London because we don't have a direct flight from Tripoli to Shannon."

"Yes, I understand that."

"Let me see what is available on those days. Would you mind hanging on for just a moment please, sir, while I check?"

No, he didn't mind hanging on. He had no intention of taking the flights. He was simply doing his job as a British Secret Service officer at MI6[1], sending coded messages through the British Airways reservations system much the same way the Pentagon used Wal-Mart's giant computers.

"Sorry to keep you waiting, sir. Yes, I can make those bookings. We're wide open on that day. What class would you prefer?"

"First class, please."

"Certainly, sir. The names of the passengers?"

"Two different names. My name: surname Lombard, as in the bank; first name, Jake. Second name, Cahill; first name, Claudia."

"Could you spell the last name for me?"

"Claudia. C-l-a-u-d-i-a."

MI6 used a special British Airways number available twenty-four hours a day. The reservation clerks were more careful than most, and the tickets were booked instantly. Each ticket had a coded number, which was forwarded automatically to the appropriate embassy, spy headquarters, or safe house. Once the information was retrieved, the bookings were automatically cancelled and disappeared from the system. Never happened.

But agents in Tripoli and Ireland knew that Joe Cahill and Jake McCabe were on the *Claudia* and that Joe was heading from Tripoli for home. And there was an account at

---

1 The Secret Intelligence Service (SIS), commonly known as MI6, the foreign intelligence service of the United Kingdom.

the Lombard bank in London that neither the Libyans nor the IRA was using. At the time, the IRA could not or would not believe the British had infiltrated them. They executed traitors. But now and then, they missed one.

And they'd missed one now.

In the dead of the Mediterranean night, the *Claudia* slipped out of Tripoli and chugged her way west off the coast of Algeria, through the Strait of Gibraltar, and into the Atlantic Ocean, where she swung to the north and headed towards Ireland, passing Portugal on her starboard side. The March days and nights were still cold while the *Claudia* plugged on.

Her two German crewmen took turns at the wheel while Joe Cahill, Jake McCabe, and Denis McInerney ate, slept, kept watch, and worried. Especially Joe. He was too old and too smart not to know when something puzzled him, ate at him. What puzzled Joe was something he thought he'd seen in the Mediterranean, just before the coast of Morocco simmered into view off the port side.

Had he seen something shiny poking out of the water? *Come on, Joe, you're getting paranoid.* But he continued to worry, even as the sea roughened and the Waterford coast of the Irish Republic was just twenty-four hours away.

***

"You what? You let them come into Tripoli? And you loaded the consignment on the docks here? Against my direct orders?" An angry Gaddafi was not a man to take lightly.

In front of him stood the five Navy supply men who had overseen the *Claudia* operation. All wore full naval dress and stood as rigid as the corpses they might soon become.

Also in the room were three traditionally dressed thugs belonging to Gaddafi's much-feared Secret Police, *Maktab Maaloumat al-Kaed.* They had been spied on during the entire operation, with cameras, tape recordings.

Not only had the five officers disobeyed orders, but Gaddafi was not yet ready to let the world know he was supplying people who were branded as terrorists with weapons, whatever the cause. But he was establishing himself as a serious arms dealer, often not for the money because he had the oil, but for ideology and sometimes, it seemed, just to be a troublemaker and irk the U.S., the Brits, and the Israelis. But he didn't want satellites or foreign spies spoiling his intentions, so he had to teach these five—and the nation—a lesson. He would put them on trial for treason.

For security reasons, no mention would be made of what treachery they had committed, but there could be only one verdict and one punishment. Gadaffi ordered them to be arrested and jailed.

As handcuffs were clamped on their wrists and chains affixed to their ankles, Ayub el-Sahafat fell to the floor with a crash, right in front of the Colonel.

Then Ayub opened his hand. In it was a note.

Gadaffi swiftly picked it up, opened it, and read: PAKISTAN. READY!

He whispered to one of the security men, folded the note, and tucked it in his robes as the five trembling seamen were led away to await their military "trial."

CHAPTER TWO

March 1973

Genius Headquarters: The White House

"What the fuck does that thieving Arab want now? Napalm and Sidewinder missiles?"

U.S. President Richard Nixon was in full rant mode. He was still smarting—if that's a word one could associate with Nixon—from his total surrender two months previously when he, along with his secretary of state and international war criminal Henry Kissinger, signed documents known as the Paris Peace Accords that led to the humiliating defeat and withdrawal of the mighty United States from Vietnam. Slanty-eyed peasants in ragged black pyjamas had out-terrorized them.

Nixon gripped the message marked SECRET in his right hand. He wheeled on Kissinger. "Henry. You're supposed to be the brains on this foreign affairs stuff. What the fuck do our people mean: 'Matters are quickly coming to a head'?"

"Well, Mr. President, I think it means that Gaddafi is changing his mind about the oil deal."

"He can't do that. When he decided to nationalize his oil fields, he agreed to leave our twenty-five oil fields alone. Guaranteed the safety of our people. He swore we could keep our airbase. What the fuck's he up to, Henry?"

"My sources tell me he's pissed off that the Israelis have a nuclear weapon. Now he wants one, too. And if we don't help him, he'll get it from someone else."

"Jesus Christ. You mean that madman wants a bomb?"

"That's what it looks like."

"Where'd he get one?"

"Well, Mr. President, he's got a lot of money. And he's got access to yellowcake."

"Yellow cake? What's that?"

"It looks like powdered flour, and as the name suggests, it's yellow. But it's really enriched uranium, which as I'm sure you know, Mr. President, is necessary in the construction of a nuclear device."

"Of course I know that, Henry. I'm not a fucking dummy. So what do we do now?"

"We could start by sending a rocket up his ass."

"A rocket? You mean a Polaris from one of our subs in the Med?"

"No, not a real rocket. A metaphoric one."

"Metaphoric?"

"A very stiff warning that we know what he's up to and we'll shove it up his ass if he goes any further."

"The rocket, you mean?"

Kissinger looked blankly at his commander in chief. *No. Don't say it. He won't get it anyhow.*

"Mr. President, leave it to me. The CIA tells me they've got someone on the inside, and he's just given them a very nice little piece of information about the IRA."

"The IRA? What have they got to do with it? Don't tell me those bastards want a bomb, too. Jesus, Henry, are they going to blow up Buckingham Palace and that prick, the Duke of somewhere?"

"Edinburgh. An atomic bomb would blow up a bit more than Buckingham Palace, Mr. President. Perhaps all of

London and the surrounding countryside, most of Great Britain, and maybe some or all of Europe."

"Europe? They'd blow up Europe? We'll have blown them up first, Henry."

Henry was tiring of the tease. It was too easy, but even he found it a bit of a worry that his president would blow up Ireland. *Note to self: Don't mention the IRA and the bomb again,* he thought. *At least, not to Nixon.*

"No, no, Mr. President. They don't want a bomb. Well, not the big one. But they do want some—how shall I say it? Trinkets. And the Colonel is providing them free of charge. Seems he wants to help terrorists."

"Did you say terrorists, Henry?"

"Yes, but don't worry, Mr. President. They're only blowing up each other and a few British soldiers. Let the Irish sort out their own problems. We don't want to get messed up with those crazies, but we can teach Gaddafi a lesson."

"How?"

"It's happening as we speak, Mr. President."

CHAPTER THREE

March 29, 1973

The March winds stiffened into a howling gale, and the seas rose and crashed over the decks of the *Claudia.* The Waterford coastline lay hidden behind the rain and mist.

"What do you say, Joe?"

"There's a bunch of lads waiting on the beach for our signal. Since the radio's broken, we'll just have to wait offshore until the weather eases. Then the lads will see us. They'll come out on fishing boats and unload the stuff."

Within twenty-four hours, the seas calmed and the fog lifted. And, right on cue, the first fishing boat came alongside and the unloading began.

Crack!

"What the fuck was that?"

Crack! Pop, pop, pop. Crack!

"Jeesus Christ Almighty. It's the fucking Navy!"

The *Claudia* was under fire from three Irish Naval Service ships that suddenly appeared, heading towards them at full speed—two minesweepers and a fishery protection vessel.

In the distance, way in the distance, a conning tower. The "stick" that Joe Cahill thought he'd seen in the Mediterranean.

It was a fucking conning tower! And it had followed them from the moment they'd left Libyan territorial waters until they reached the Waterford coast. The Irish Navy was tiny. It didn't have one submarine.

Cahill quickly surmised it must have been British, probably one of their newer nuclear-powered Dreadnought class. Cheeky bastards. But it was all over. The IRA men and women onshore melted away. Navy officers boarded the *Claudia* and put her and the crew, including Cahill, under arrest and hauled them away. Cahill wondered if he'd removed all the Libyan identification on the satchel. Yeah, he was pretty thorough about that.

An alert Irish officer thought he'd seen a package, maybe a briefcase, flung over the side, but a diver found nothing. However, a local "fisherman," a member of the IRA, had also seen the package go overboard and nonchalantly dropped a buoy to mark the exact spot. A couple of days later, when the furor had subsided and most of the cops had gone, the fisherman sailed to the buoy and, with a grappling hook, dragged up the mysterious object. It was a briefcase. Gaddafi had stuffed it with fifty thousand British pounds. It also contained false passports and the names of future contacts for the IRA throughout Europe and the Middle East. And the Navy had missed it. *Ooooh.*

Cahill got three years' jail; the others, two years. When he was sentenced, Cahill was as defiant as all IRA leaders who had gone before him.

He proclaimed to the Irish Special Criminal Court: "If I am guilty of any crime, it is that I did not succeed in getting the contents of the *Claudia* into the hands of the freedom fighters of this country. And I believe national treachery was committed when the Irish Free State forces conspired with our British enemies to deprive our freedom fighters of the weapons of war."

Two days after the *Claudia* left Libya, the five supply officers were seen on television throughout the country. It was a show trial. They had betrayed the revolution, and traitors must pay the full price, according to Allah, praise be upon Him. It didn't matter that the Muslim holy book, the Qur'an, didn't say a word about executing Navy supply officers who had fucked up a little as opposed to a huge catastrophic lot. Nor did it mention the IRA. Perhaps a quick rewrite in a Pakistani madrassa would help the modern Muslim steer his or her way through the perils of the new world. If the *Oxford English Dictionary* can eliminate hyphens, clearly nothing was sacred.

About to be eliminated in Tripoli this day were five human hyphens who had pissed off the accuracy-obsessed Colonel.

Bang. Bang. Bang. Bang. Wait! That's only four!

What happened to the other *bang*? On his way to London already, spared for the moment because he had promised to get his boss two atomic bombs, one for him and one for Pakistan.

***

The chief petty officer, Ayub el-Sahafat, sipped on chilled Dom Pérignon in a first-class British Airways seat that had been booked under a false name.

Passport? He snickered. Who was he this day? Maybe a fucking Jordanian. Yeah. Nobody would suspect a Jordanian. That *Claudia* thing was almost a disaster. Still, what did he care? It was probably just reaching Ireland, and he was headed to London where a bank held five million pounds for him. He'd have to set up other accounts in, say, Hong Kong and New York to cover a few tracks. How much would the Pakistanis pay? And what about his friends in Washington?

"Yes, please. Another glass of champagne."

It was fun being a spy. It really was.

"Salam alaykum."

"Wa alaykum as-salaam, how was your flight?" The first secretary, Ahmed Amin, from the Libyan Embassy in London smiled broadly as he warmly greeted Ayub at the arrivals gate at Heathrow. "Here, let me carry your bag, old friend. The embassy limo is just over here."

The black Mercedes with the diplomatic plates eased away from the curb.

From another corner of the complex, two other vehicles also emerged. One, a non-descript grey four-door, mid-size sedan; the other, a blue van, with a sign on each side that read: JIFFY PAINTERS. WE'LL BE DONE BEFORE THE PAINT DRIES! It, too, was fitted with the strange little communications block on the back of the roof.

"So where would you like to go? I think the ambassador should meet you, and then perhaps we can check you into the Hilton on Park Lane. Not too obvious, but nice just the same. Oh, and you have an appointment with a bank manager in the morning at ten thirty," breezed the First Secretary.

The chauffeur flicked his eyes from the road to the rear-vision mirror. "We've got company."

"Have we, now? Know them?"

"No. Never seen these ones before, but they're rigged out like the Brits."

"Okay. Why would they be following us today, do you think?"

"Are you asking me?" Ayub asked.

"Yes. You haven't been up to anything silly, have you?"

"Me? Of course not. I'm sure you heard about the boss getting mad about letting a damn cargo ship come into the harbour."

"Oh, I heard about that all right. Everyone did."

"What do you mean?"

"You haven't seen today's papers, have you?"

"No. Why?"

"Take a look."

The Chief Petty Officer froze. *Oh god! No!*

"You weren't very careful, were you?" The First Secretary was no longer smiling. A grim hard stare had replaced his easy smile.

The Mercedes sped up and turned sharply down one side street, then another.

"Read what it says!"

"But I didn't know!"

"Read it!"

"IRA SHIP AWASH WITH LIBYAN TERROR WEAPONS."

First Secretary Amin pointed to another headline. "This one!"

"LIBYAN TERROR SHIP CAUGHT BY IRISH NAVY."

The Chief Petty Officer wouldn't appreciate the irony. The Taurus 9mm was a handgun his Colonel often shipped to the IRA. Gun experts praised the Brazilian-made Taurus 9mm for its excellent use in short-range combat, its well-designed trigger, its weight and size. In later years, it would get a reputation in the United States as an excellent "concealed carry" weapon. Nor would Ayub be overawed by the statistic that the bullet hit him travelling at over seventeen hundred feet per second with a muzzle thump (that's how hard it hit) of a thousand pounds of kinetic energy.

Yes, it hurt. Very much. Almost as much as when Ayub's head hit the pavement after the First Secretary shoved him out of the speeding Mercedes—along with the gun that had been fired from a gloved hand. It *should* have hurt. But the Chief Petty Officer didn't feel a thing. The moment he saw the headlines, he knew his career would be better in Korea—the north, that is. Anywhere but in the backseat of a speeding car with a Taurus 9mm about to re-arrange his rib settings.

***

The morning papers confirmed the First Secretary knew his job: IRA GUN KILLS MAN IN BROAD DAYLIGHT.

The carefully-worded press handout was carried by most of the British and international media:

> A man, possibly of Arab descent, was shot and killed in the West End yesterday. Police say they have reason to believe the man, whom they think is about thirty years old and who has not been identified, was shot with a 9mm handgun commonly used by the Irish Republican Army. They refuse to say why they believe the IRA is connected with this particular murder weapon.
>
> Eyewitness said that at about 3:45 pm, at the corner of Brompton Road and Beauchamp Place in the Knightsbridge area near the Libyan Embassy, a black limousine, possibly a late-model Mercedes Benz, was seen turning the corner at a high speed.
>
> "I saw the door open and a man fly out onto the road," said a witness who did not want to be identified.
>
> Police say they have contacted the Libyan Embassy and a spokesman has denied any knowledge of the event. However, because of diplomatic privilege, the embassy will not allow police to inspect any of their vehicles or interview embassy staff.
>
> An autopsy will be performed later today to confirm the cause of death. Police say they have not found any connection with the murder and the seizure yesterday of the arms ship, *Claudia*, near Waterford in the Republic of Ireland. In the seizure, the Irish Navy found five tons of weapons and ammunition and arrested five men, including the alleged IRA Commander, Joe Cahill. But they say among the weapons were a number of Taurus 9mm handguns.

What the papers and police did not say was that two other vehicles—a mid-sized grey four-door sedan and a van with JIFFY PAINTERS adorning its sides—along with an ambulance and a fire truck had raced to the scene. Nor did the police say to which hospital the victim had been taken.

CHAPTER FOUR

Flash-forward one year, to help put perspective on the gruesome follies of man and, some would say, beast...

May 18, 1974

India was having a bad morning. It was about to set off its very own nuclear bomb. It had just thrashed Pakistan in its third war and was on a high. But suddenly there was a hitch in their strictly coordinated plans. The schedule dictated that at precisely 8:00 a.m. in Rajasthan Desert, India would test what it wanted the world to believe was its very first "peaceful nuclear explosive," a great oxymoron, but the Indians persisted in kidding themselves and even dubbed it the "Smiling Buddha" bomb. Happy, smiling, chubby, nice, cuddly A-Bomb. Okay. Only don't be surprised if it goes *boom!* with a bit more cheerful energy than anyone could imagine. And it was all to be kept a secret.

Shhh. Don't tell a soul. No one will ever know an A-bomb has gone off. Nah.

Well, it almost didn't go off. An engineer's jeep broke down right beside the bomb. *Oh dear. What do we do now? Blow him up, too? Oh no, think of the paperwork.*

The army rescued the scientist and the jeep. At 8.04, the electronic detonation system team leader, Pranab Dastidar, pressed the button and up went an eight-kiloton bomb. The scientist then tried to contact Prime Minister Indira Gandhi hundreds of miles away in New Delhi with their glorious news. But they didn't succeed. The dumbfounded geniuses couldn't get their top-secret line to Delhi to work. They could detonate an atom bomb but couldn't figure out the complexities they, themselves, had built into it. One of the scientists got on his rickety old bike and wobbled the two kilometres into a nearby village to make the call, but he'd forgotten the number and hadn't bothered to write it down. An officious and suspicious village operator didn't believe this buffoon should talk to the office of the Prime Minister of India and refused to connect him. But after half an hour of cajoling and a wad of rupees, the operator relented.

Mrs. Gandhi was not amused at being kept waiting. Had something gone wrong?

"Why didn't you phone me from the bunker when you were supposed to?"

"No, no, there was nothing wrong, just a last-minute hitch, ma'am, with the 'neutron path beryllium initiator.'" Gibberish to a nuclear scientist, but it shut up Mrs. Gandhi, and her annoyance quickly turned to delight.

An address to the nation would be the least she could do. It had been a mere two years since she had told the scientists to proceed with their secret research and make the so-called "peaceful bomb."

But as the ultimate team leader, Raj Ramanna, observed later: "The test was a bomb; an explosion is an explosion. A gun is a gun whether you shoot at someone or shoot at the ground. I just want to make it clear that the test was not at all peaceful."

Hearing the news across the border, the Pakistani prime minister, Zulfikar Ali Bhutto, promptly soiled his crisp white salwar kameez. He waddled off to clean himself and had a thorough ponder as he squatted, just to ensure there were no more surprises. Nope. He had his own nuclear power plant provided by that queer chap Trudeau from Canada.

Ali was no patsy. He knew which side the breed was Bhuttoed on. After consulting with his eldest daughter, Benazir, he told a group of trusted scientists he wanted to go "that extra step," too, especially after his troops had received such a shit-kicking in Bangladesh from that fucking Hindu Rahman.

Bhutto would become famous. He would produce the world's first Muslim bomb. Allah, praise, and all that stuff be upon Him. But that bitch Indira Gandhi was way ahead of him. She might even take Kashmir.

Bhutto pondered a little more. *I think I need to make a few phone calls. China? North Korea? No, I'll start with Gaddafi, but I'll be careful with that deceitful bastard. What's that Libyan proverb? "They sell the monkey and laugh at the buyer"? Well, here's one monkey-seller that won't be laughing. And didn't Gaddafi say he had a man posing as a Navy officer?*

***

"Mr. President, we have some news from India."

"What? They've just found out how to use paper to wipe their asses? I tell you, Henry, that was the funniest thing I've seen in my life. Remember? The motorcade roared through those fucking great puddles in Delhi. Showered them as they were taking a shit. Christ, that was funny."

"Yes, it was very amusing, Mr. President. But this is a little more serious."

"What, they're still using their hands?"

Nixon was irrepressible. He was on his fourth rum and Coke and it always went straight to his addled brain faster than he could utter another expletive.

Kissinger despised his crudeness and his intellectual inferiority but never more than when Nixon was drinking—which was every night. And every night he got drunk, he threatened to blow up the world, including Ireland.

"Mr. President, no. No, don't pour yourself another one just yet. Mr. President, India has detonated a nuclear weapon."

"That fucking clown in a loincloth? Spinning, spinning—what the fuck was he spinning? I thought he was one of those Beatnik peace-types. Henry, what was that song?"

"'The Spinning Wheel Ride'?"

Nixon grumbled the words and danced a little step. "Bloody sweat and tears, huh, Henry? That's what Churchill said. He knew a thing or two about sweat and tears."

"No, it's not the man in the loincloth. He died twenty years ago. His name was Mahatma Gandhi. Mr. President, why don't you sit down for a minute? Listen to me very carefully. India has detonated an atomic bomb."

"Jesus Christ, Henry! Why didn't you tell me? You're my secretary of state! You must tell me these things, Henry! Was it that scrawny little bastard in a loincloth? Henry? I never trusted the little fucker."

"That's because you never met him. He's dead. Mr. President? Mr. President? Oh god, he's passed out. Hello. Get me the Chief of Defence Staff. Seth? Henry. He's passed out again. Don't launch any goddam planes or missiles even if he insists he's the President. Just say the usual: 'Yes, sir. I'll just check the co-ordinates, and they'll be on their way.' Then call me back. I'll get Nancy to give him a shot. He won't remember a thing in the morning. Thank you, Seth. Oh, India? You've heard? Yes, very hard to miss. Oh, about seven kilotons, our boys reckon. That's what I wanted to talk to Nixon about. Yes, you're right, Seth. Pakistan won't like this one bit. Oh well. Goodnight, Seth. But call me if he asks you to blow up Ireland or kill a man in a loincloth. Ah, long story. Goodnight."

Kissinger poured himself a brandy, ignoring the grunting, heaving heap on the sofa who would, in just three months, resign in disgrace as the thirty-seventh president of the United States. But right now, he had to deal with that "old witch" Gandhi, a term both he and Nixon had used to her face. How dare she deal with the Russians and the

Chinese? All non-aligned meant was you were pro-Commie and anti the United States.

"But now she's got a bomb," Kissinger mumbled. "Hmm. She kept that one pretty quiet."

CHAPTER FIVE

May 19, 1973

The howling of hot air and the screeching of brakes told the chauffeur and the hundreds of others jammed on the platform that the next train was about to grind to a halt at Knightsbridge Underground Station.

Yuseff Hussein had changed out of his driver's uniform and into shirt, jacket, and jeans but still looked like an Arab to the browsers and buyers from Harrods and adjacent luxury boutiques. He was headed home near Finsbury Park. The others? To places much grander, even if they took the Piccadilly Line.

Although he worked for the Libyans, the chauffeur was Algerian. He was forty. Lived with his wife and two teenage kids in a small flat not far from Finsbury Park Station. He'd lived in London for ten years and had started out as one of those freelance mini-cab drivers, so he knew his way around. The Libyans liked him and had sent him to a special school for chauffeurs just outside of London, which taught defensive driving, evasive tactics, and curiously, he thought, what to do in a kidnapping.

Often, on his way home, he would stop off for a pint at the King's Head, a pub on Blackstock Road. He liked the warm British beer that came from kegs, not the fancy bottles from Europe or Ireland. Sometimes, he'd pick up a copy of the *Evening Standard* and flip to the football pages to see how his favourite team, the "Gunners"[2], were doing. Not that he didn't know down to the last away-goal, but he still liked to read about it.

So, just before going into the pub, he slipped the right change for the newspaper to the vendor outside in his little kiosk, folded the copy under his arm, went in, nodded to the barman whom he vaguely recognized, and asked for a pint of the best bitter.

"Oh, and a packet of crisps. Feeling a bit peckish tonight. It's been a long day."

"Okay, guv. Salt and vinegar all right with you?"

"Yes, fine."

He gave the bartender a five-pound note, waited for his change, and left a tip. "And have one for yourself."

"Cheers, guv, don't mind if I do."

The Algerian moved to a vacant table. Not too many people in the pub: an older couple in the cheap red-backed chairs in the corner, two men drinking pints at the bar, two younger women with cocktails a couple of tables to his right. The pub wasn't what you would call cozy; it had been taken over by one of those brewery chains that made all their properties look more or less the same. Not drab, but not that welcoming, either; its lights were too bright. The TV above the bar was tuned to a silent game show.

But the pub suited the Algerian. It was near home, and it gave him a breather at either end of the daily sardine rush. He took a sip of beer and unfolded the newspaper to the front page.

No one seemed to notice as he sputtered and choked slightly on the beer. So the boss *killed* the little guy! He'd thought he was just winded.

---

2 Arsenal Football Club, English professional football (soccer) team based in London, England.

"Oh my god!" Hussein mumbled. He'd seen it. Would they come after him? No, wait. Probably nobody saw him. He was going pretty fast. And the embassy kept out the cops. But they could track him down. All they had to do was check London embassy drivers. All of them must have security passes for the palace and Downing Street. "But I didn't do anything," he muttered. "I was too busy driving the limo." But what about those two vehicles that were following them? *Oh my god! I saw the van with the paint sign before the ambulance passed us! That's right!*

The Algerian trembled. He took another sip of beer but spilled a little. And then he did a very rare thing. "Ah, mate, could I have a scotch, please? Make it a double."

"Are you all right, guv? You look a bit queazy."

"Oh, yes, thank you. Think I'm coming down with a cold. Thanks."

As he sat again, the Algerian paused and stared out through the frosted patterned windows of the pub. It was getting dark, but he thought he'd seen something familiar. A van. It had just driven slowly past the pub. He thought—thought—he saw JIFFY on its side.

He quickly downed the beer and the scotch, got up, hurriedly left the pub, and walked towards home. He kept on the south side of Blackstock Road, in the shadows when he could, turned left onto Ambler Road, and broke into a slight jog when he crossed over towards his house on Romilly Road. A quick look over his shoulder, and he hurried on. No sign of the van. He must have imagined it. He almost grinned at his foolishness and slowed to a walk.

***

A passing jogger found the Algerian's body the next morning on the edge of Finsbury Park, not too far away from the pub. Four minutes by van, to be exact. Little remained of his head, which had been drilled with five 9mm bullets. The same number of bullets found in the chamber of the Taurus handgun. The police tape extended an unusual twenty metres out from the body, keeping nosy onlookers too far away to see any details.

An ambulance woman covered the body with a sheet. She and her partner lifted the body onto a stretcher.

She seemed a little surprised when a senior cop covered in braid, accompanied by a shorter man in plain clothes, spoke to her. From a distance, it looked as though they were arguing.

Then, from the far side of the park, a van appeared. It approached the group front-on and stopped beside the ambulance.

The Algerian was lifted into the back of the van, which swung away, heading back in the direction from where it had come. But, as it turned, one word came into view: JIFFY.

****

"How's he doing?" MI6 boss Malcolm Forbes-Smythe was at his most emetic, solicitous best as he oozed concern to First Secretary Amin, both standing a disrespectful twenty yards away from the rib-riddled patient in London's Guy's Hospital.

"Oh, he'll be okay. His ribs will hurt like hell for a few days. Those blank bullets are far more lethal than you'd think. They can take your eye out. A Hollywood chap was playing Russian roulette with a 457 Magnum blank and ended up dead. But it's the concussion your boy suffered when you rolled him out of the limo that we'll have to watch."

"Well, Gaddafi thinks he's dead, and that's the main thing."

"But he can't remain dead forever, if you know what I mean."

"Yes, he's got a lot of work to do. Get the Pakistanis a bomb and get one for Gaddafi. How are we going to arrange that?"

"We might need to ask the Yanks to help. Oh, by the way, I hear your driver never made it home last night."

"Oh, so that was you?"

"Not me personally, dear boy. But it had to be done. One never knows who's working for whom these days, does one?"

"I guess not. But what about the police?'

"No problem there. The Chief Superintendent actually belongs to us. Which reminds me. Your Chief Petty Officer has five million pounds of ours sitting in Lombard's bank. I think, under the circumstances, we'd better get it back before anyone else tries to remove it."

"Five million pounds? Why so much?"

"Cost of doing business, dear boy," Forbes-Smythe said. "Especially if you're buying and selling bombs. Your man was saying he needed a lot more. He wants to buy off a Pakistani nuclear fellow in Belgium or Holland. Says the man's a genius. Reckons he can get him to sell his secrets to Gaddafi and, at the same time, arrange to take possession of this yellowcake stuff Bhutto wants. He's going to be a busy boy when he wakes up. I do so hope he doesn't get greedy or we'll have to put a stop to him, too."

"But won't Gaddafi go ballistic when he finds out he was fooled?"

"Not ballistic, dear boy. Nuclear. He'll go nuclear and that is our Chief Petty Officer's life insurance. Neat, what? In the meantime, we'll let the Colonel play his little games with the IRA and the Palestinians. We don't care too much about them. But now that the Israelis have their Dimona bombs, they need—how shall we say—persuading not to use them. So our persuasion would be Gaddafi and Bhutto. Two Islamic bombs as opposed to one Jewish."

"What about the Hindus?"

"Yes, well, that's another reason we want your boy to get better. Now, care for some lunch? MI6 does a splendid toad-in-the-hole. Rather appropriate, what?"

"Ah, I've never had it before. This frog in the hole."

"No. No. Toad, dear boy. Toad."

"You mean they cook the toad?"

"No. No. It's just a name. Looks like toads sticking their heads out. It's really quite delicious. Sausages in batter and lots of fried onions. Some folks find it a bit greasy, but I think you'll love it. Delicious."

"*Nek ni,*"[3] the First Secretary muttered.

"What's that you said, old boy?"

"Oh, nothing. Just an old Arabic phrase of thanks to Allah, praise be upon Him, before we eat."

"Oh, how very nice."

Nek ni.

[3] Mainly Gulf slang used throughout the region. *Nek ni*: fuck me.

CHAPTER SIX

June 1973

Ennismore Gardens is a posh address, surrounded by cobblestone mews within ethereal echoes of Monteverdi madrigals emanating from the nearby Brompton Oratory. And the home of not just playgirls and playboys, such as Babs Streisand and Hugh Heffner. It also housed, albeit in the basement of number fifty-nine, a journalist well-known in the Arab world, Mustaffa Fakih, who was reading the agency wire copy and frowned.

As the seasoned senior London correspondent for the popular Egyptian newspaper *Al-Ahram*, Fakih knew the best stories were sometimes those little ones that didn't make much sense. The ones that skirted over the details and quoted some spokesperson or other but stopped without revealing much of anything. Sometimes they were planted by the police or the government. Other times, they were exactly what they appeared to be: badly written, badly reported stories of little consequence.

But this one felt different, he thought. *There's something else going on. Call it instinct, call it experience.* Fakih knew what he had to do as a good investigative reporter—begin the maddening, frustrating job of trying to join the dots.

The news item he had just read simply said that a man had been found murdered in Finsbury Park. His body had been taken away for an autopsy, and his next of kin had been informed. A bartender at a nearby pub said the man was a regular customer. When he'd served him the previous night, he'd looked frightened or ill. He thought the man, who was an Arab, was a driver of some sort because he sometimes came into the pub wearing a chauffeur's uniform.

An Arab in a chauffeur's uniform? Hmm, Fakih thought. Had he worked for any of the embassies? Wasn't that Libyan who was killed the previous day thrown out of a black limousine? Was that an embassy car? Whose? And the story mentioned the IRA. The gun, that's right. The same type used by the IRA? Why would they say that? And that shipment they caught in Ireland. That was the IRA smuggling guns from Libya. What the hell was going on?

Fakih decided to first call the Finsbury Park police to see if they would tell him any more.

"I'm sorry, sir, but that's all we've got to say."

"Can you tell when you will release his name?"

"That will probably come from Scotland Yard."

"Why is that?"

"Sir, as you know, the deceased was a foreign national, and in cases like this, the Yard has to do some checking before giving out any more details."

"Can you tell me what nationality he was?"

"I don't think there's any harm in that," the officer said. "He was Algerian."

"The newspaper said he might have been a chauffeur."

"Yes, I read that, too, sir, but I cannot confirm that detail."

"Can you tell me the name of the pub he went to? I'm going to have to check them all anyhow. But you might be able to save me a bit of, how you say, shoe leather."

"It's the King's Head. But that is all I can really say. But, I must say, sir, I'd hate you to waste too much of your time. To me, it doesn't look like anything more than an armed robbery that turned into a homicide."

"With five bullets to the head? Isn't that a bit unusual?"

"Now that you mention it, Mr. Fakih, I think you're right. But everything is getting more violent these days."

"Yes, sadly you're right, officer. Thank you very much for your time."

That cop didn't know much, Fakih thought. Scotland Yard?

He looked up the number and dialed.

"Scotland Yard Press Office. Constable Mavis Dorling speaking."

Fakih went through the niceties.

The cop in the press office was distant and cold. "No, we have no information to release about this incident."

"Can you at least tell me when you will be releasing the name?"

"No, I can't."

"Just one more question, please. If someone threw a murdered body out of a diplomatic car in central London, would that be reported to you?"

"Of course," she snorted.

"Then can you give me some information about the man who was killed in Knightsbridge? The newspaper quoted the police as saying the gun used was the same type used by the IRA."

"That statement did not come from this office," she said.

"Uh, where did it come from, then?"

"In matters of terrorism, all statements are issued by the Home Office or the Foreign Office."

"Do you know which one?"

"I repeat, in matters of terrorism, all statements are issued by the Home Office or Foreign Office."

"You're not going to tell me?"

"All statements in matters of terrorism are issued by the Home Office or Foreign Office."

"Thank you, Officer Dorling, you have been most helpful."

What did he know so far? The man in the park was probably an Algerian chauffeur. Drank alcohol, so he wasn't a strict Muslim. But even the cop thought five bullets to the face unusual. That bitch at Scotland Yard jumped a mile when he mentioned the IRA. But why the problem about releasing the Algerian's name? Sounded as if the police weren't talking to each other. Unless... Unless it was the Special Branch or the Secret Service. That would make sense. No trouble proving that, he thought sardonically.

Fakih put on his coat, closed his door, and walked into the rain. He was in luck. Even near Hyde Park corner on a late wet afternoon, he managed to hail a taxi.

"The King's Head Pub on Blackstone Road in Finsbury Park, please."

Fakih entered the pub and ordered a lime juice cordial and soda.

"Okay, guv. Cor, look at tha' wevva."

"Yes, the weather's terrible." But Fakih's mind was on other things. "You think he was a chauffeur? The man who was murdered."

"Yeah. Poor blighter. Who'd have done a thing like that? His poor wife and kids."

"Wife and kids?"

"Yeah, they live not too far from here. A relative was in earlier trying to find out if he'd been in last night. I said yes, and they said do you know what time, and I said yes about seven o'clock, and they said when did he leave, and I said about half an hour later, and they said how did he look, and I said he looked as though he'd seen a ghost and left here in a hurry and—"

"Sorry to interrupt, but did you catch his name?"

"Who? The relly?"

"Yes, and the dead man."

"Yeah, because they wanted me to help them write his death notice, so I went over to the bar and—"

"Sorry. Sorry. What was his name? The dead man."

"'Ang on. Here it is. Yuseff Hussein. Of seventy-eight Romilly Road."

"How far is that from here?"

"About five minutes, guv. You know, it's a funny thing, though. Romilly Road where he lives is near the back of the tube station, so what was he doing way over the other side of Finsbury Park? That's what I'd like to know. It's in the opposite direction."

"He might have decided to go for a stroll before going home."

"Don't think so, guv. He went out of here right quick, he did. And I saw him turn left out of the pub. He was going home. But in a bit of a hurry, if you know what I mean."

Fakih knew what he must do next. First, talk to the family. That would not be easy, even for an experienced reporter like him. Then he would have to take a look at the murder site and talk to the Finsbury Park cops. That might have to wait until the next day. It was still raining and getting dark. But he was onto something.

"How do I get to Romilly Road?"

"Easy, guv. Turn left out of the pub. Stay on this side of the street until you reach Ambler Road. Then walk down to Romilly Road on your right."

Fakih paid for his lime juice cordial and soda, gave the barman a nice tip, got his name and telephone number, and stepped into the London night.

Now to the family of Yuseff Hussein, he thought.

It took him just over five minutes to reach the darkened terraced house. Hard to tell if anyone was home. He rang the doorbell. He heard what sounded like a shuffling of feet coming down a staircase, and the door slowly opened.

"Are you the police? Where is my husband's body?"

Mariam Hussein looked beaten and robbed. Fakih guessed she was about forty and about five feet two inches. Her headscarf didn't fully cover her greying hair. Her lined face and reddened swollen eyes gave her a look of intense despair.

"No, I'm not the police. I'm Mustaffa Fakih from the newspaper *Al-Ahram*. That's the big one in Egypt. Mrs. Hussein, first let me say how terribly sorry I am."

"The police said I shouldn't talk to any reporters. You'd better go away."

"Mrs. Hussein, did you say you didn't know where your husband's body is?"

"They won't tell me. He should be washed and buried by now. I want him to go to Allah according to our Muslim traditions. He would have wanted that, too."

"Mrs. Hussein, I don't think the police are telling you the truth about your husband, and I'd like to help."

"They said he was murdered. Why? Why would anyone kill my husband? And why was he in the park? Where's his body?"

"Mrs. Hussein, may I come in so we can talk inside? Then no one will know you've spoken to me."

The grieving woman sobbed quietly as she opened the door a little wider and led Fakih upstairs to her flat. There, she would tell him a story he could not have imagined.

A story not for the weak.

CHAPTER SEVEN

Mid-1973

The city of Almelo's official guidebook is honest—or stupid enough—to opine that Almelo is not a highly remarkable city in the eastern part of the Netherlands and has only a few interesting sights to offer. It even describes *itself* as one of the most boring towns in Europe, if not the cosmos, and its fifty thousand dreary residents agree.

Almelo was trying to compete with its bigger brothers and sisters (near the German border) when it came to shopping and entertainment, but unfortunately, it failed. For dazzling nightlife, other places were definitely better: Hengelo or Enschede.

The Kreta Restaurant stood on Klara Zetkinstraat, an eternally long street name that served only to locate the unlikeliest short meeting place for two strangers passing by the site.

"So what's a nice Muslim boy like you doing in a dump like this?" the American tourist asked.

"I work at Urenco," Abdul Kadeer Khan said. "I'm a scientist there."

"Urenco. Urenco. Don't they have something to do with atomic stuff?"

The thirty-seven-year-old Muslim was more talkative than usual, although still careful. He'd just received news that he'd obtained his Ph.D. in metallurgical engineering from the Catholic University of Leuven in Belgium. He was in high spirits for a lonely scientist and didn't mind chatting to the fat, middle-aged American tourist, who'd said he was pedalling his way across the country.

"Say, we didn't introduce ourselves. My name's Bob Cartwright. From Sacramento, California. And you?"

"Ah, they call me A.K."

He had just told a little white lie. Yes, he worked at Urenco, a consortium that made nuclear equipment. Almelo was its main enrichment site, and A.K. was stealing all the secrets he could find. Secrets that would soon make him a very rich and very wanted man.

"I must get back," Khan said. "Nice talking to you. Enjoy your trip."

Cartwright left A.K., hopped on his bike, and headed down the street named Weerselosestraat. When he reached the Hotel Jachtlust, where he was staying, he leaned his bike against the fence and entered the hotel. He needed to call Amsterdam from his room.

After reaching his room and ensuring the door had locked, he picked up the phone.

"British Airways? I'd like to make a reservation. London to Amsterdam on the fifteenth. And, also, I'll need a rental car at Schiphol Airport and a hotel in the town of Almelo. Two nights at the Hotel Jachtlust. Almelo. Alpha, Lima, Mike, Echo, Oscar. That's it. My name is Khan. Initials A.K. Right. I've got a special code for the ticket charge. Oh, you've already got that? Fine. Thank you."

Bob Cartwright was CIA. He worked a lot with MI6. This job sounded like a real doozy. He'd heard that mad bastard Nixon—or was it Kissinger?—wanted him to go to Chile to kill Allende and put some thug Pinochet in power. *Huh? No way.*

But what about this new order from Schlesinger? Bob had just gotten the job as head of the CIA Foreign Liaison, and Schlesinger was ordering Foreign Liaison to tell him about any "operations outside the organization's legal charter." Schlesinger would shit himself if he knew about the two bombs the Brits were cooking up for Bhutto and Gaddafi. Fuck. He'd go nuts. Well, no one would tell him. "I'll make fucking sure of that," Cartwright muttered.

And how long would Schlesinger last? About a long as Nixon, he reckoned. The Watergate Hotel. *Man, talk about amateurs. You want a break-in? Hire a pro. Our guys would have been in and out of there in a flash, and no one would have ever known. So why does Schlesinger think we did it? Because he's a dickhead, that's why.*

Cartwright got off the bed and looked at the phone. He had to find out.

"Could I have Saint Michael's Hospital in London, please?" He rhymed off the number and was connected.

"Hello. Saint Michael's? Could I have the special care unit, please?"

"Special Care."

"This is Dr. Cartwright. I'm just inquiring about my patient." Bob Cartwright did a great balancing act. He managed to sound like a real specialist while knowing the fewest of medical terms, most related to the female anatomy.

"He's out of the coma and doing very well. He's a little confused but that's just the medication. He'll be up on his feet and back to work in a day or two."

"That is good news." He really, really believed it.

"Oh, and Dr. Cartwright, we received the background information you phoned in earlier today. It was just what we needed."

"I'm glad. I'll visit my patient tomorrow if that's all right?"

"Fine. I'm sure he's got a lot of questions."

"I'll bet he does."

"Bye, now."

St. Michael's Hospital, my ass. The Brits put on a great act. Well, I've got a plane to catch.

***

"So Mr. Khan's in Holland. Odd that he should go to Almelo," Malcolm Forbes-Smythe, the head of MI6 said.

The MI6 boss liked and trusted Cartwright, a fat, friendly American who despised his bosses but didn't want to get out of the spy game. So he free-lanced for the British without telling Langley Headquarters in Virginia all they might have wanted to know.

"Yeah, he's got an office there and is supposed to be just consulting," Cartwright said. "He doesn't have special security clearance to get to see the guts of the enrichment operation at the Urenco plant, but my guess is once you're in, you're in."

"What makes you think Khan is our man?"

"I watched him for a few days. Each morning he'd arrive right at nine o'clock carrying a slightly battered black briefcase. Didn't seem to be much in it. At lunchtime, right at noon, he'd go around the corner to the same café every day for lunch. That's where I made sure I accidentally ran into him that one time. He spent about a half hour on the patio writing in a small pocket-sized notebook as he ate. Then he'd go back to work. He'd come out again at five. But twice the briefcase seemed to be a lot fuller than when he arrived. I took some long-range shots to show you."

"Did you turn his flat over when he was at work?"

"Uh huh."

"And..."

"How much are you guys paying me?" Cartwright asked.

"Probably too much. In Irish punts. Rhymes with..."

"Hunts. As in, I went on a hunt and found a suitcase under Mr. Khan's bed."

"And being a good, law-abiding spy operating illegally, committing an illegal act in a foreign country, you didn't open it and took it straight to the local police."

"Funny bastard, aren't you? Do you want to know what was in the suitcase or not?"

"I presume you have it on microfilm?"

"Here you are."

"What is it?"

"I checked with one of your eggheads before I got here. He had a look. Like all oh-so-fucking-funny Brits, he just said: "So when do you intend to detonate this bomb, Mr. Cartwright? Please don't do it next Thursday. That's my day off, and I don't want to be disturbed. And would you mind not doing it near Torquay. My dear mother lives there, and the noise of a ten-kiloton nuclear device going off would upset her terribly."

"Sixteen kilotons. So our Mr. Khan has been stealing plans from Urenco?"

"Yep. Your egghead comedian suggests that Khan has made drawings of all the facilities right under their noses, written up extra notes at lunchtime, and then back after lunch for more. He reckons Khan has now got complete plans for an installation and complete plans for a bomb. A do-it-yourself atomic bomb programme."

"For Pakistan?"

"Who else? But there are duplicates and triplicates. Maybe Mr. Khan is going into business for himself, as well as Pakistan."

"He could sell a kit to anyone with the right amount of money? Even the IRA?" the now-deeply engaged head of MI6 asked.

"Could be. But I don't know what his price would be. A shitload, for sure."

"How much is what you Americans call a shitload?"

"If I had what he's got, I'd say ten million dollars."

"Hey! That small Libyan friend of ours, who by the way is fully recovered apart from being very angry and delighted at the same time, well, he has five million pounds sitting in Lombard's."

It was Cartwright's turn to worry. "You mean we buy Gaddafi's bomb for him?"

"That way we control the Colonel's—how shall we say—extra-curricular activities. Even get him to drop one on, say, Belfast if it ever got out of control."

"You fucking joker! You'd never drop a bomb on Belfast."

"Not me, dear boy. The Colonel."

Cartwright's face whitened. "You would, wouldn't you?"

"Not me. I'm not allowed to do that sort of thing. Her Majesty might have questions. Oh dear no, we couldn't have that. Blowing up her beloved six counties and probably half the other part of that dreadful place, too. Just wouldn't do, old boy. Not terribly British, you know. But Gaddafi, well... They say he's mad."

"You know, sometimes you scare even me."

"Good. Keeps you on your toes. Now, this Mr. Khan. We should pay him a visit. Or perhaps our Chief Petty Officer would like a little trip. With that small amount of savings he has in the bank. You should go with him just to make sure he doesn't do anything silly, like double-cross us or make a run for it. If that happened, well... You would know what to do."

"Kill him?"

"Both of them. But if you get caught, we've never heard of you. Deal?"

"And if I say no?"

"We'll have you, how shall I say, meet the same fate."

"You know what? I actually believe you. You would take me out, too."

"Oh, Bob, you Americans are so melodramatic. But in a nutshell, dear boy, yes."

***

Malcolm Forbes-Smythe exuded the aura of the British upper class to which he clearly belonged. He had buggered at Eton, rogered at Oxford, muff-dived for England. He wore superbly tailored suits, silk shirts, and spankingly good ties worth many glittering solid gold sovereigns. A man of impeccable background and grooming. He had served with the elite SAS[4] where he learned to kill in top-secret operations in Yemen.

One of his first jobs as Britain's chief foreign spook was to infiltrate the IRA. The lad he'd picked for the job, Billy McFadden, was also in the SAS but still had a thick Belfast accent. The false documents showed Billy had been kicked out of the Army for stealing weapons and selling them on the black market. For that, his "records" showed he had served two years in Brixton prison.

When Forbes-Smythe first approached the Provos in a pub on Falls Road in Belfast, they were casual and pretended to know nothing. But they were suspicious. Especially after Forbes-Smythe introduced them to his plant. Then left.

Billy McFadden simply ordered a round of Guinness, and the tension dissipated like the froth. Almost.

"So you were in the Army, Billy, were you? You don't look like you've been in the Army. Your hair's too long, and you don't stand up straight," Joe McGuigan said.

"Those fuckers," Billy said. "They put me in Brixton for two years."

"They did, did they? Well, yes, we heard. Nice wee guns."

John McGuigan, the commander in chief of the Belfast Brigade, was still alive because he was no fool. This could be the Brits trying to get in.

"So, Billy, are you up for a wee job tonight?"

Already? If they've fingered me, I'm dead.

"Meet me after the pub closes."

"Where?"

"Just walk along the road. We'll find you."

Billy had a choice. Make a run for it, or stay and either die or join the IRA.

He walked out of the pub. The few streetlights left after years of rioting cast dim, menacing shadows. Billy knew he couldn't run. He had his orders.

---

4 Special Air Service, a special forces unit of the British Army, founded 1941.

Crack! A gun barrel whacked him on the back of the head. Billy went down without a sound. Four masked men roughly but efficiently hauled him into a small house.

Billy woke, feeling only a massive pain in his head. As he slowly came out of his fog, he realized two things: a pistol was pressed against his temple and he was naked.

"Now, Billy, we've searched your clothes, taken your picture and your fingerprints. What do you have to say now, Billy boy?" McGuigan said.

"Oh Jesus, that hurts. If I didn't check out, I'd be dead by now, right?"

"Right, Billy. So now that wee job."

While Billy dressed, McGuigan told him of the plan. "Every night at around one, a black taxi drives by. It has different plates on different nights, but the boyos inside are always the same. My lads tell me they are British spooks from MI6 taking photos with night lenses. They've even got a camera hidden in the grille. And they've got this fucking new space-age device that hears through walls. They stop every couple of nights and have a listen. We want them out of the way, and that's where you come in, Billy."

"What do you mean?"

"As your initiation into the IRA, we want you to kill those three English bastards."

"Tonight?"

"Tonight, Billy. The taxi always slows down when it turns left from the Falls into Leeson Street. A minute or so before it appears, an Army jeep does the same thing, making sure there are no surprises. Tonight, Billy, you'll be the biggest surprise of all."

Kill my own men? Fuck! "What weapon will I use?"

"Here you are, my son."

Billy recognized the "Widow Maker" as soon as McGuigan took it out of his bag. An ArmaLite AR-108. Armour-piercing bullets leave the nineteen-inch barrel at five hundred feet per second. This one had a magazine of thirty .223 caliber bullets, capable of firing seven hundred of them every minute. It was the IRA's favourite weapon. Rugged, light, and unstoppable at a close range.

"I've never used one of these, Mr. McGuigan. We used M16s. Should we wait a couple of nights so I can get the feel of this thing?"

"Not trying to get out of this, are you, Billy? That would be awkward."

"No, no, Mr. McGuigan, but each gun is different, and I want to do the job right."

"You'll have no trouble, my son. Just spray those bastards, and we'll get you out of there before you can say 'fuck the Queen.' Quick. Now. We'll get in place just in case they changed their plans."

Billy felt the vomit surging in his gullet. He'd killed men, even kids, but they were sanctioned targets. They weren't his brothers-in-arms. *Don't puke, for Christ's sake! Don't puke! Oh Christ, I'm going to shit myself. Remember your training! Squeeze your buttocks together. Don't shit yourself!*

They gave Billy a black balaclava, and all five left the house by the back door, scuttled across the yard, hopped two fences, and stopped in a dark alley beside the corner of Falls Road and Leeson Street.

Ten minutes to go.

The five masked men waited in disciplined silence, hidden in the dark alleyway.

McGuigan leant in front of Billy and flipped the safety catch to "off." McGuigan didn't want any excuses. If their Billy fucked this up, he'd be ex-Billy, traitor. They'd find his body way down in Crossmaglen, a village in Northern Ireland, shot dead in "bandit country" by the IRA because they'd have used the ArmaLite. Those bastards in London would know the IRA got their quisling.

The whine of the jeep announced its presence.

"That's them, boyos! Billy! Take aim, but hang back until you see the taxi."

McGuigan sensed the kill. He shouted his whispers as his heart rate jumped. God! This would be good. Three dead fucking Special Branch.

Billy's pulse raced, too. But in dread. He had to kill them. He had to. But could he?

The jeep, covered in anti-riot meshing, rounded the corner. The driver and a soldier wearing night goggles sat in the front. Two squaddies in the back were aiming their rifles. The jeep slowed, turned the corner, and stopped. Right beside the alley.

The driver was on the radio. The soldier with the night goggles peered down the alley.

The five masked men flattened themselves against the wall.

Seconds later, they heard: "Romeo Tango Romeo Tango. Think we saw some movement in an alley on our left just after we turned into Leeson Street. Wait for my all-clear."

Oh Jeezus, Billy thought, *they're going to come down the alley!* He heard the men beside him pull what he guessed were weapons from their belts.

The two squaddies, with miner-like lamps on their helmets, slid off the jeep and, with rifles in firing position, eased into the alley.

Suddenly, hands clamped the two men's mouths. After a stinging in their necks, they fell to the ground. Their throats had been perfectly slit.

There was commotion from the jeep. "What was that, sir? Did you hear that scuffling noise? Where did Wilson and Marcus go?"

"I didn't see anything. They must be further on down. We'd better check."

"Romeo Tango. We are leaving the vehicle. Do not proceed until I give word."

The two officers in the jeep opened the doors.

This time, McGuigan didn't wait.

Puff. Puff. The silencer never failed.

Both Brits were hit. One died instantly. The other, the commander, lay in the alley as blood trickled down his nose. He looked up at McGuigan and tried to speak. Then his eyes dimly focussed on Billy. "Don't I... Don't I...?"

He got no further.

McGuigan stood over the dying officer, looked down at him, spat, and fired one more bullet into his head.

"Jim, the jeep!"

Jimmy O'Donnell, an amateur actor, ran over to the vehicle, picked up the radio, and in his best British accent passed on the news. "Hello, Romeo Tango. Acknowledge, please."

"Romeo Tango. Here. Anything wrong? Over."

"Ah, Romeo Tango, nothing wrong. Routine check. All clear for you to proceed in five minutes. Over."

"Roger."

In the alley, awash in blood and littered with four dead British soldiers, the IRA men got to work. They were well-prepared, and in a guerrilla war, simple solutions were always best. Earlier, they had parked two wheelbarrows against the wall. The locals knew not to touch or steal anything the IRA left around. The barrows were meant for the MI6 spooks, but they came in handy now. Two bodies were dumped across each other and wheeled to the jeep.

O'Donnell rammed the gears into drive and screeched away from the alley, sped down Leeson Street, took a sharp left, and turned into an IRA safe-garage. He pulled down the door. He'd drive off again in five minutes before the Army swarmed in looking for their missing men. This time, Jim would set the jeep ablaze in Protestant territory to throw the Brits off the track.

Billy had been so busy helping with the bodies that he forgot about the taxi. And the Colonel.

McGuigan was still suspicious. "That fucking Brit seemed to know you, Billy."

"I don't know him. But he could have been on a training course with me when I was in the Army."

"Aye, you could be right. Are you ready, Billy? That'll be the taxi I'll be hearing."

The steady throb of the taxi neared. Billy raised the ArmaLite to his shoulder and peered through its night sights. In thirty seconds or so, he would have to kill his own men or have his throat slit. *No way out now, Billy.*

Billy had no more time to ponder. The hulking cab chugged around the corner, running on its parking lights.

Billy had thirty rounds of ammunition. *Single shots? No! Flip it to automatic!*

"Billy! Now! Shoot the fuckers now!" McGuigan screamed.

Billy obeyed military orders at all times.

Crack! Fuck! They shot me! My upper left shoulder.

"Shoot, Billy. For fuck's sake, shoot."

Wild instinct kicked in. Billy pulled down on the trigger and charged the taxi, spraying bullets, blowing out windows, killing three of his comrades.

O'Donnell screamed up behind the taxi in his jeep. The three dead MI6 men were dragged into the jeep and dumped on top of the other bodies.

Amazingly, the taxi was still running. Michael O'Harahan jumped in, got an ass full of glass and blood, and raced across the Ardoyne area, into a deserted unlit field. The sirens were wailing as they threw matches in the petrol tanks and ran like hell.

The blood from the slit throats had splashed onto Billy, McGuigan, and O'Donnell when it cascaded out of the soldiers. More dangerously for the killers, their shoes and boots were soaked in blood and would leave tracks easy to follow. All the footwear had been bought in the Edgeware Road in London, so it would be possible to trace.

"Dump the boots and socks! Take them off away from the blood," McGuigan ordered.

Barefoot, two of the masked men hustled the injured and trembling Billy down a short flight of steps into somebody's kitchen, opened a trapdoor, and entered a tunnel. They must have crawled for what seemed like an hour until they emerged into a darkened hall in Andersonstown. A light flipped on. A church—they were in a fucking Catholic Church!

Among the statues of the Virgin and other saints appeared a silhouette framed in the flame-flickering Belfast night.

"Father O'Grady here has studied medicine. He'll take care of your shoulder, Billy."

"That I will, Billy. You've just been grazed. Would you like me to hear your confession first?"

***

Malcolm Forbes-Smythe's phone rang at 3:20 a.m. "God!" he muttered. He rolled over Jeremy and picked up the receiver. "What time is it? What do you want?"

"Sir, it's Tommy Beecham." Tommy was Forbes-Smythe's private secretary and a distant cousin of the famous British conductor. Tommy never missed the last night at the proms nor any performance of the Delius *Requiem*. Sir Thomas, as did Tommy, had gone to Oxford, but he'd taught himself how to conduct an orchestra. Tommy did not teach himself how to help run MI6, but he knew how to conduct himself at a time such as this.

"What is it, Tommy?"

"A car is on the way, sir. Should be at your door in twenty minutes."

"That bad, Tommy?'

"It would seem so, sir."

Jeremy stirred slightly. "What the hell's going on? Would you please turn the light off, Malcolm?"

"Sorry. I have to go. Spy stuff, you know."

"Fuck me." Jeremy sighed in frustration at being woken in the middle of the night.

"Not now, Jeremy. I have to rush."

Malcolm's flat straddled the rococo borders of Knightsbridge and Kensington. But even here, his palatial address couldn't disguise massive prices and minute corridors. Deep, deep, deep in thought, he headed for the bathroom, still perplexed by the phone call.

Forbes-Smythe could have used his secure line, but if Tommy didn't want to risk even that being intercepted, it had to be bad, he mused as he quickly showered and dressed.

Exactly twenty minutes later, the doorbell rang. It was Tommy. MI6 used its own staff to drive its bosses around at night. Tommy would have strapped on a Glock 23 pistol, and in the green Rover that followed, two plain-clothes cops would be armed with heavier weapons.

Traffic was heavy at any hour of the day or night in this area that dripped with silent Rollers and flamboyant Bentleys screaming: *Look! Look at me! I'm so indubitably rich! Get out of the way, you nasty little people!*

Even amid this sacrosanct armada, the red MI6 Morris Mini looked like a million other Minis, except this one was souped-up and bullet-proofed. Tommy kept it right on the speed limit as he wheeled around Hyde Park Corner and headed towards Vauxhall Bridge. They could talk about football and the weather but not the reason for the nocturnal journey. That was a rule. Recording devices were too easy to plant.

Ten minutes after they left Prince's Gate, the little red Mini crossed Vauxhall Bridge, turned left, and drove into MI6. The green Rover flashed its lights and sped off.

Malcolm all but ran into his Temeraire, which was what he'd dubbed his office in honour of the Turner masterpiece painting[5] that hung over his opulent mahogany desk surrounded by leather sofas. HMS *Temeraire* had achieved mythical status for its decisive role in the Battle of Trafalgar in 1805 and has maintained its stature as a symbol of British military might. So smitten with the myth, Malcolm fantasized about changing his name to Malcolm Forbes-Temeraire. Bit much, perhaps? Even for Malcolm.

"So what is it, Tommy?"

"Belfast, sir. Seven British soldiers dead. The bodies are badly burned, but first indications are that three of them were ours."

"Jesus. The taxi run?"

---

5 *The Fighting Temeraire*, an oil painting by the English artist Joseph Mallord William Turner, painted in 1838.

"Yes, sir. The taxi and the lead jeep were both burning like hell when the RUC[6] got there. At first, they thought it was the Prods because the vehicles were found near the Shankhill, but the military went over the route and found an alley at the corner of Leeson Street and the Falls. And blood. Lots of blood."

"So it was the IRA."

"For sure, sir. But what's unusual about it—you know we deliberately set up the patrol to lure them out—was that they weren't coming. And if they had, we were ready. We took all the precautions. So what happened? And why tonight?"

"Tommy, when did Billy arrive in Belfast?"

"Last week, sir. He made the phone call as arranged. He said he was joining the health club."

Forbes-Smythe smirked at the coder's irony. Some clubs were better for one's health than others.

"Tommy, did he say when he was joining?"

"Yes, sir. Tonight."

"You don't think the IRA tested him so quickly?"

"Our people in Belfast say McGuigan is very antsy these days. Getting more ruthless, too. But if they suspected Billy, he'd be dead."

"How do we know he's not?"

"We don't, sir. We haven't heard from his shadow."

"Why the fuck not, Tommy! It's his fucking job!"

"We're trying to reach him right now, sir."

"Trying? Why the fuck hasn't he called in?"

"I imagine the place is crawling with cops and Army and everyone's listening in on everyone else. I know we are. So he probably doesn't want to risk it just yet. He's a good chap. I imagine we'll hear from him as soon as he thinks he can get a secure call out."

"I suppose so. Jesus. Three of ours. Do we know them?"

---

6 The Royal Ulster Constabulary, the police force in Northern Ireland from 1922 to 2001.

"No, sir. They're still identifying the bodies. I'm told they're locals, but they went through training with all our folks. First-rate, I'm told, sir."

"And we don't know how they were killed?"

"Not yet, sir. But our own lab boys are on the scene so we should know that quite soon."

"Um, Tommy, a thought has just crossed my mind. If—just if—it was Billy who killed them, that's one British subject in the employ of Her Majesty's Intelligence Service killing three of his fellow officers. And I ordered him in. Couldn't this be legally tricky?"

"It's what we'd call murder, sir. And yes, you would be responsible because you ordered the infiltration. Technically speaking, that is."

"But Billy never asked for clearance to kill his own men, did he?"

"No, sir. Would you have given it?"

Forbes-Smythe paused. *To get in and get to the top of the IRA? Damn right I would.* "I'm not that callous, Tommy. No, I would've told him to wait or get out of there. We'd have to try another time."

"I think you're right, sir. Human life is precious even if we are at war with terrorists."

CHAPTER EIGHT

Twelve hours later, a weary Forbes-Smythe sighed heavily as Tommy ushered in Chief Petty Officer Ayub el-Sahafat, the chief of supplies of the Libyan Armed Forces, and Bob Cartwright, chief of his own skin. The Temeraire was setting sail into quite uncharted waters even though it overlooked the Thames and was just a few treacherous nautical yards from London Bridge.

Earlier in the day, Billy's shadow did call from Belfast, who confirmed Billy was in, and Malcolm surmised, but could not confirm, that Billy's initiation did include killing the men in the taxi. It had been sprayed with thirty bullets from an ArmaLite rifle, and the operatives died of multiple gunshots to almost every part of their bodies. On the other hand, the four soldiers in the alley were killed singly and methodically, all pretty much at the same time.

Let's see how far he can go. The top would be good. Must make sure the police investigation gets contaminated so nothing leads them anywhere near Billy. The IRA can have this one for free, Malcolm decided magnanimously.

The "crew" of Malcolm's Temeraire plopped and slopped down on the leather sofas for this important meeting. An emergency meeting, really, but one Malcolm deemed an hyperbole inapposite on this brooding, cloudy London morning.

"Sorry about your boys, Malcolm," Bob Cartwright said almost honestly. "Anything I can do?"

"No, but thank you, Bob. It never gets any easier, does it?"

"Hey, what about me? How about apologizing to me. You almost had me killed!" Ayub el-Sahafat was still pissed off about the fake shooting and the rude ejection from the speeding Mercedes.

"Be thankful, Ayub, that I needed you for something or I would've had you killed, okay? Once we seized all those weapons on the *Claudia* and took that charming Mr. Cahill away, I could've had you sent back to face Gaddafi, and your neck would've said farewell to your cranium before you could say Allahu Akbar."

"Why didn't you?"

"Well, as you know, we British are a grateful lot, and you did persuade us to put a nuclear submarine on the case, as it were. Gave the lads on board quite a kick. Better than fucking around playing wargames with the Greeks and the French. They're jolly grateful to you, too. Now, about that five million pounds in Lombard's—"

"That's my money! It is part of my expense account. I told you Gaddafi wants a bomb."

"Ayub, do you know the current price for a black-market bomb?"

"Four million?"

"Not even close, dear boy. Not even close. And unlike you, we know where we might get one, and we'll even throw in the extra cash," Forbes-Smythe said.

"To help Gaddafi get a bomb? Why?"

"His bomb will be our bomb. Yes, yes, we've got plenty, but your Colonel has none. So we'll make a deal with him. We—you—will get him his little toy, but we will tell him where and when to use it."

"Mr. Malcolm, forgive me for saying this, but I think you are fucking crazy. Gaddafi will never go for a deal like that."

"Ayub, I think I know your Colonel better than you do. He'll make the deal with the full intention of double-crossing us. Once he has the technology, he'll hire some crazy North Koreans to build a secret facility and a secret bomb, thinking we won't know anything about it."

"What would you do?"

"Simple, dear boy. Destroy it and your Colonel and take back his bomb. Or, should I say, our bomb."

"Kill Gaddafi? You'd never get near him," el-Sahafat said.

"No, but you could."

El-Sahafat suddenly felt his bowels loosen. He crossed his legs tightly and, in so doing, severely crushed his right testicle.

"In pain, old chap? How about some tea? Tommy, be a good lad and get the Chief Petty Officer a nice cup of tea. Bob, you want one?"

"I hate that English shit. Isn't it about time you opened the booze cabinet?"

"As my darling father used to say, 'Not until the sun's over the yardarm.' Never knew what the old queen meant. I think he should have said 'under the yardarm.' To use your dreadful American terminology: 'whatever.' What would you like?"

"Scotch on the rocks."

"This is ten-year-old Glenmorangie and you're asking me to fill it with gravel?"

"Ha, fucking ha. Ice, you asshole. Ice."

"That's even worse than rocks. You'll have it with a splash of soda. Neat, or not at all. Now, how would you like it?"

"Just fill the fucking glass, Malcolm!"

"Manners, dear boy. Manners."

"All right. Please fill the fucking glass."

"I'd like one, too," el-Sahafat said. "This tea tastes—how do I say?—like kitten's piss."

"Cat's piss, dear boy. And no, you can't have any. You're a Muslim, and I won't have you committing sacrilege in my office. How are the balls, by the way?"

Ayub momentarily considered punching this English prick in the mouth but remembered the Mercedes and changed track. "How do I get the bomb?"

"Oh, the bomb. Bob, why don't you lay it out for the Chief Petty Officer."

Cartwright took a deep gulp of whiskey. "Ever heard of a Mr. A.K. Khan?"

"Khan. Khan. Yes. I know his name. I also know a dance called the can-can. French girls in frilly knickers. I saw them once in Paris. Oh, they were so beautiful. You know, the women in Libya are not so beautiful. They're all covered up. Such a shame."

The little bastard's horny, Cartwright figured, even with sore balls. *Ah, give the man a drink.* Cartwright gave the Arab a stiff one.

"Think you should meet him," Cartwright said. "By the way, do you know anything about yellowcake?"

Forbes-Smythe interjected before it got silly. "He means uranium ore, not a wedding cake."

"Yes, of course I know," Ayub el-Sahafat said. "Niger's got a ton of it."

Niger, on Libya's southern border, is a Muslim country of roughly twelve million people and an endless supply of uranium.

"How do you know our Mr. Khan?"

"You sent his name on the BA system."

"Who gave YOU access to that?"

"A friend of Mr. Bob's."

"Dear god! Bob."

CHAPTER NINE

Mariam Hussein poured the Arabic coffee into small clear glasses. Her flat was rented and badly furnished. Two cramped bedrooms; a bathroom with an ever-running toilet; a scuffed and chipped bathtub without a shower; a grimy, dimly-lit kitchen; and a dining room with an old mottled green sofa, a bare wooden table, and four plain wooden chairs. A postcard and a stick of rock candy still in its wrapping—souvenirs from Brighton—sat on the mantelpiece over a coin-in-the-slot gas heater. A tapestry of a phrase from the Qur'an was the only ornamentation on the damp-looking brown wallpaper.

"Where are your children, Mrs. Hussein?" Fakih asked.

"I sent them to their grandmother's in Algeria one month ago."

"Why?"

"Mr. Fakih, my husband was not just a chauffeur. He gathered information, too."

"He was a spy?"

"No. Not him. But the Algerian government is very suspicious of Libya and its close ties with Tunisia. It wanted better information."

"And Mr. Hussein got it?"

"Yes. He listened very carefully to all the conversations in his car. He sometimes secretly recorded them. And sometimes he even copied documents on the Libyan ambassador's desk."

"But if he wasn't a spy, what did he do with the information?"

In the musty cold room, Mariam Hussein paused. She looked down in deep thought. Then she looked up again and began to take off her hijab. She unwound it slowly, first slipping it off her head, then away from her neck.

Fakih stared. Gasped. "My god, who did that?" He was looking at a massive scar that encircled her entire neck.

"There are more on my back and ribs."

"Mrs. Hussein, what happened?"

"I was just a young girl, about twenty years old. It was during the war with the French. I ran messages to the FLN[7] resistance fighters, but one day I got careless. I dropped a message right beside a French soldier. He had stopped me to ask for my papers. They did that all the time. But when I dropped the paper, he picked it up. I started to run as fast as I could up the street. He yelled at me to stop or he would shoot, but I didn't stop. He missed me, but I tripped and hurt my ankle. The French threw me in a car and took me to prison. A man came into my cell with a torch. Is that right? Torch?"

"What kind of torch?"

"One that had flames coming out of it."

"A blowtorch?"

"Yes. Yes, that's it. A blowtorch." She paused and stared at the wall. "That's when it began. 'That's a very pretty necklace you have on,' the man said, fingering it lightly. The necklace went all the way around. It was like the ones the West now vulgarly calls an Algerian love knot."

"So then what happened?"

"He asked me for names and addresses of FLN members, but I refused. So he lit the torch with his cigarette

---

[7] Front de libération nationale, the only constitutionally legal party in Algeria (1962-1989).

lighter. A huge flame shot out, and he held it very close to my neck. It was so hot. He asked me again, but I refused to talk. He moved the flame closer until it touched the necklace. I still refused to talk. I could feel my whole neck burning. I started to scream, and the necklace got hotter and hotter. It felt as though my whole head was on fire. I could smell my skin melting. I could feel the necklace sinking deeper into my throat and all around me. I was going to die. The Frenchman screamed at me that the necklace was red hot. 'Talk! Talk!' he screamed. And I just screamed in pain. Agony. I don't remember any more. When I woke up, I was in some kind of hospital with tubes and bandages. They had beaten me while I was unconscious. My legs and back were so very sore. Allah must have wanted me for another mission because I got out of the hospital without any more beatings but with these terrible sores and scars. They took a year to heal, and now I'm left like this."

"So you hated the French."

"Mr. Fakih, I vowed to somehow get even with them for what they did to my country and me. Did you know a million people died because of the French? It wasn't until Yuseff and I and the kids moved to London did I find my way."

"What was that way, Mrs. Hussein?"

"When Yuseff got his job as a driver for the Libyans, I would chat to him about his day. And he would tell me all about the big shots he was driving around. Yuseff overheard one of them talking about Libya getting something called nuclear fission. He didn't know what it meant. I found out."

"And when you found out, what did you do with the information?"

Mariam Hussein wrapped the scarf back around her neck and over her head. She was silent for several long moments. "Forgive me. It takes time for the images and the pain to go away. I feel the pain still."

Fakih said nothing. He imagined the toll it took on her whenever she talked about the incident. He sipped the lukewarm coffee and waited.

"Mr. Fakih, please do not judge me. I am sure they killed my husband because they thought he was the spy, but that is not true. My poor Yuseff died because they must have thought he was the one passing on the secrets to the Algerians. But it was me. When Yuseff told me about the conversation about nuclear material, I asked him to see if there were any documents he could get hold of. The ambassador had left London for a week, and Yuseff volunteered to paint the inside of his office. They are cheap, the Libyans, despite all their oil money, so they said yes. Stupidly, no one guarded the office, and in the end, Yuseff came across two dossiers that spelled out Libya's intention to get a bomb. He photocopied them and put them back."

"And he gave the copies to you? What happened next?"

"This is the incredible part. I took the tube to the Algerian Embassy in Holland Park and asked to see the ambassador. I showed the people at the front desk my neck, and the next thing I knew, I was being escorted into his office. I started to tell him my story and what I had seen. He interrupted me and called in another man and a woman. I suppose they were secret agents. Then he asked me how much money I wanted. I was shocked. I wasn't doing it for the money, and I told him so. I said we should steal Gaddafi's bomb when he gets it or steal his plans and make our own bomb. If Algeria had the bomb, the French would never have another day of peace. They would be terrified we might use it against the great republic. And think of the glory it would give to an Arab country with a nuclear weapon."

Fakih had finished his coffee but kept sipping on the empty glass. He was working out the terrible possibilities.

"The ambassador thumped the table and said Libya must never get the bomb. He said I had to stop them. Me? How could I stop them? By getting more information. They insisted on paying me five hundred pounds and made me promise not to tell anyone."

"So why was Yuseff killed?"

"I think the Libyans must have done it. And the British helped them."

"Why would the British help the Libyans?"

"Mr. Fakih, I do not know. I do not know."

"Why did you send your children to Algeria, Mrs. Hussein?"

"In my years in the resistance, I was trained to be a lookout and to know when I was being watched. Mr. Fakih, there was a van parked along this street day and night. It had some kind of sign about being painters. But I never saw anyone paint anything. Sometimes there was a man in it. Sometimes two. It started just days after I went to the Algerian embassy. I did not like it. They were watching this house, so I sent the children away. Then they killed Yuseff. I must be next."

"Not if they think Yuseff was the spy. You're probably still quite safe."

Fakih didn't believe a word he'd said, but he knew he had stumbled on a story. A big story.

How big, he had no idea.

CHAPTER TEN

It was raining when Chief Petty Officer el-Sahafat and Bob Cartwright reached Almelo. The private flight from London had been delayed so they were running late. It was already lunchtime, and Mr. A. K. Khan would not be on the patio but inside, transcribing his secret notes.

"How will we recognize him?" el-Sahafat asked.

"Are you serious? You two will be the only dark-skinned people within a fucking million miles. So if it's not you, it must be him."

"Funny bastard, aren't you?"

The Libyan had recovered some of his—and how he would hate this word—chutzpah, especially with five million pounds in cash hidden in a very large waist belt.

Cartwright suddenly jammed on the brakes, and the Libyan almost rocketed through the windscreen. The American wrapped el-Sahafat in a crippling headlock and could have killed him within seconds. What Cartwright knew, but el-Sahafat was blissfully unaware, was that heavy pressure on the carotid sinus nerve at the side of the neck, just above the shoulder, can cause what is known as carotid sinus syndrome, resulting in dizziness, fainting, and convulsive seizures. At the same time, pressure on the carotid artery resulted in a dangerous slowing of the heart rate. Cartwright was doing both.

"Malcolm doesn't care if you live or die. Someone else can take over this project. Watch your fucking mouth, and don't ever abuse me again! Don't ever forget your place! Okay?"

"Okay. Okay. Sorry, Bob. Sorry. Jesus! You almost killed me. Now, where is this restaurant?"

It was about a block away. The patio tables had been folded away in the gloomily drenched little town. The restaurant itself was quaint enough: white stucco pillars at the entrance and tulip boxes adorning pretty rounded windows. Bright candelabras inside made it look even cheerful.

They strode to the entrance where a waiter approached them when they entered.

"Heb je een tafel voor zes?" Bob tried to show off his Dutch. He shouldn't have. He'd just ordered a table for six.

"Six or two?" the waiter asked in flawless London-accented English.

"Two, of course."

"You said six in Dutch. I could give you a table for six if you really want. One person at each end. You could pretend you were having a banquet."

"Why would we do that?"

"You Americans like big things, don't you? By the way, why are you with such a short friend? I can get you a much taller one if you want."

Cartwright wasn't sure whether the waiter was taking the piss[8] or just being friendly. Either way, he was an asshole.

"Hey!" el-Sahafat whispered. "That's Khan."

The Pakistani was ladling soup into his mouth, but he appeared to be concentrating so hard on writing that he lost synchronization. He missed his mouth and spilled scalding

---

[8] A British term meaning to mock at the expense of others, or to be joking, without the element of offence.

pumpkin puree onto his crotch. He squeaked and rubbed his crotch furiously. This was the man who held the future of part or all of the world in his, well, hand.

Cartwright approached Khan's table. "Say, bud, if you want to do that, you should go to the bathroom."

If Khan's skin wasn't so dark, Cartwright would have seen the scientist glow a brilliant red.

"Oh, no. No. Excuse me, I spilled my soup, and I was trying to wipe it off my trousers," Khan explained.

"Sure, bud, sure. But it looked to me like you were slapping the salami."

"No. I'm having soup and a chicken sandwich. No salami."

"You were choking the chicken, then?"

"The chicken is dead. It is cooked. See?" After pointing to his sandwich, Khan examined Cartwright's face. "Say, didn't we meet a few weeks back?"

"Yeah, sure. I was on my bike. Now, don't tell me. You said to call you A.J. No, wait. A.K.! Right."

"What an excellent memory you have. I am so sorry I have forgotten your name."

"Bob. Bob Cartwright. And this is Mr. el-Sahafat. Do you mind if we join you?"

"Well, I was just finishing off some notes and—"

"Notes, Mr. Khan? That is your name, isn't it? A.K. Khan?"

"How did you know?"

Cartwright almost taunted this Islamic infidel. "Let's just say my friend and I have an interest in you."

"Who are you?"

"Oh, we're just a couple of guys travelling through town. You work at Urenco, right?"

Jaw drop! *Sirens*! Bob, the trained observer and sometimes assassin, sent instant flashbulbs to Khan's brain. By the expression on his face, it was obvious he didn't like this one bit.

Cartwright wondered if Khan thought they were cops, or maybe Khan thought they were Urenco bosses. Was he worried that someone at Urenco had seen him making drawings?

Khan slowly slid the notepad into his pocket.

"You were writing on the notepad last time I saw you," Cartwright said. "What are you writing?"

"Oh, I don't think that's any of your business."

"Ayub, why don't you show Mr. Khan why we think it is some of our business."

Before Ayub could flash his wad of notes, the waiter appeared. "Have you decided what to order?"

"Have you got any fish in?" Cartwright asked.

Khan missed his mouth again, this time decorating his shirt.

"Yes, sir. We have some very good North Sea cod. And believe it or not, we do make great chips or, as you Americans call them, fries."

"I'll have the same," Ayub chipped in.

"Who are you people?" Khan asked again after the waiter left.

"Put it this way, Mr. Khan, we could be your very first customers. But let's not do any more business here. Why don't you come to the hotel at six tonight. Bring some, ah, evidence of your product, and we will have a generous reward for your hard day's work. Deal?"

"How do I know this is not a trick. A setup?"

"If it were, Mr. Khan, you would have been arrested weeks ago. No, it is not a setup. It could be the start of a very, very profitable business venture for you and us. But let me warn you, Mr. Khan, now that we have made contact, you will be watched. One false move, and you will be dead. So don't try to run, and don't try to give us phoney documents. We pay very well. But we also kill just as well. So tonight at six, then?"

"Yes. At six," Khan said as he got up and left.

Bob thought he walked a little unsteadily.

CHAPTER ELEVEN

"Mr. President," Kissinger said, "I think we'd better call in Schlesinger."

"Is he any relation to you, Henry?" Nixon asked.

"No, why?

"Well, your names sound the same, and you have a silly accent."

"Henry sounds like James to you, Mr. President?"

"Not your first names, Henry. Not your first names. Jesus, I sometimes wonder if I'm the only goddam person around here who gets it."

"Oh, you'll get it all right, Mr. President."

"Get what, Henry?"

"What you so justly deserve, Mr. President."

"Why, thank you, Henry. That's mighty kind of you. Now, why should we call in the foreigner Schlesinger?"

"The Defence Secretary is no more foreign than you or me, Mr. President. He's an American."

"Yes, but he's got a foreign name. I don't trust foreigners, Henry. They're not like us."

"I have a foreign name and, as you say, a silly accent."

"Yes, but everyone knows you're a bloody foreigner even if you are an American. You see the difference, Henry? So why do we need to call him in, anyway?"

"I've heard from our London embassy that the Brits have been very busy this week. They've got someone inside the IRA already, and we think they've started negotiations to buy an atomic bomb."

"Not from that little fucker in the loincloth, Henry?"

Kissinger eyed the heavy gold eagle paperweight on Nixon's desk and imagined pounding Nixon's head with it until his brains could be spread on toast.

"No, this time the contact seems to be a Pakistani."

"A Paki! What the fuck would a Paki know about an atomic bomb? They're stupid people, Henry, and devious. Remember that asshole Kenyatta? Fucking beard and beads and all that Paki shit."

"No, he was from Kenya, Mr. President. Not Pakistan."

"No, Henry, I think you're wrong there. What was his first name? Something stupid like Hambone. Why would he have a name like that if he's a Muslim? They don't eat ham, do they, Henry?"

"His name was Jomo."

"Like Jomo and the whale?"

Exactly, Mr. President. Jomo and the whale. You certainly know your Bible."

"But why does this Kenyatta asshole want a bomb? Pakis. Never trusted them."

"Mr. President, why don't I get you another rum and Coke?"

"Now, that's the only sensible thing you've said all night, Henry. That fucking Kenyatta better watch it or we'll bomb the bejeezus out of him. What do you mean 'they've got someone in the IRA'? Henry, does that mean we can't bomb Ireland?"

"I'll get you another drink, Mr. President."

CHAPTER TWELVE

Khan climbed the steps to the Hotel Jachtlust, slipped on the wet concrete, and fell headlong into one of the bushes that decorated its rustic exterior.

"Machood!" the normally reserved scientist blurted. He would never be caught yelling "motherfucker!" in his own country, but he was nervous and knew the men waiting for him would not be impressed if he arrived covered in leaves and grass.

Cartwright and el-Sahafat heard the commotion and peered out from their second-storey window.

"It's Khan, I think. Hope the little fucker's not drunk. No good dealing with drunks, Ayub."

"What should we do if he is?"

"Beat the living shit out of him, steal his plans, and tell him to come back tomorrow when he's sober."

"Here he comes now. Seems to be walking steadily enough. But just in case..."

Cartwright checked his Glock. He wouldn't kill Khan. Just whack him about a bit.

The room telephone rang. Cartwright picked it up.

"Front desk here. There's a Mr. Khan to see you. Should I send him up?"

The stupid fucker used his real name!

"Yes, please."

Minutes later, a *tap tap* at the door.

Khan, now bereft of leaves and bush, stood in the doorway. He was carrying a bulky briefcase.

Cartwright couldn't smell any liquor. "Have a nice trip?" he joked.

Khan looked a little bemused. "It is only a short walk. It was fine, thank you."

"No, I mean... Ah, well, let me get you a drink. Scotch okay?"

"I'm sorry. Thank you, but I am Muslim."

"Yes, I know. So would you like a Scotch?"

"A large one, please."

"And I suppose this other devout Muslim will have the same?"

Ayub nodded. "With ice. Rocks."

"You mean Kaaba stones?" Cartwright laughed. "That's funny."

"We do not mock Holy Mecca," Ayub said.

"Bullshit. You're doing it right now. But what the hell. Here's to our new partnership, and let's hope we make a bomb!"

"Oh, I can do that for you, sir. It just depends on the price." Ayub unbuttoned his shirt and his belt.

Khan glanced at his fellow quarter-pissed Islamic colleague as if he feared he was about to be shafted.

But Ayub simply removed his money belt, unzipped it, and pulled out a thick wad of one-hundred-pound notes.

Khan's I.Q. was 180. But not even with a brain like that could he calculate the riches that lay before him in crisp body-temperature cash. "How much do you have there?" His voice had gone up half an octave, and the booze and the billions collided in perfect harmony.

Even Cartwright was surprised at the effect of the money on this greedy little man, whose eyes had narrowed with ecstasy.

Khan's hands trembled. He took another gulp of the forbidden nectar and held out his glass for more.

"Not yet, Mr. Khan. What we have here is a deposit. But before I tell you anything more, I want to know exactly what you are selling and exactly how much you are wanting."

"It depends on many things, Mr. Cartwright. Who is the ultimate buyer? When does he want it? Does he need the parts, or will I have to arrange for them to be acquired? Does he have the expertise to build a plant, or do I help him there, too. How many bombs does he want to build?"

"So you're selling a do-it-yourself kit or an I-Khan-do-it-all kit?"

Even A.K. got this one.

"Yes. Yes, that is exactly right, Mr. Cartwright. I Khan do it all. You Americans can be very funny. Now can I have another Scottish, please?"

"Would you prefer one in a kilt or a wee lassie from Loch Ness?"

"No, I meant another Scottish whiskey."

"Oh, why didn't you say so? You can't. We haven't finished our business."

"Mr. Cartwright, I have something you want very badly. I will not give it to you until I get money and another Scottish."

Cartwright decided to show Khan who was in charge. He whipped out his Glock and rammed it into Khan's forehead. "Don't fuck with us, Mr. Khan. One shot and you'll be found a thousand miles from here very dead and very poor. The papers will say a secret nuclear weapons syndicate you had set up murdered you in a double-cross. That's what you've done, isn't it, Mr. Khan?"

"Please. Please. Put the gun away. I will co-operate with you, but I seem to have had an accident."

Khan had released a glass of the Scotch into his underwear, and it was seeping through his light brown trousers.

"Oh, I know how to get the stain out," a suddenly helpful Ayub volunteered. He grabbed a full bottle of thoroughly chilled club soda from the fridge and poured it over Khan's long- (well, quite small, really) suffering crotch.

Khan shouted the word they'd heard him yell in the garden: "Machood!"

"Bless you," Cartwright said.

"Here is the deal," Khan explained, shifting in his chair to let the chill out of his soaking scrotum. "I have blueprints here for a nuclear plant that would be capable of producing two warheads a month. I will sell you the plans for twenty million dollars. If you require the full services of myself and several colleagues to install and produce a bomb, that will cost sixty to one hundred million dollars. But please do not think I am stupid. The plans I have brought with me tonight are missing vital components. I will first need a deposit."

"But don't you need more than money? The Chief Petty Officer here says you have been looking for a constant supply of yellowcake."

"That is correct."

"The bosses in Pakistan know what you're up to?" Cartwright asked.

"They do not care as long as I get Pakistan an atomic bomb. Or, as we prefer to call it, the Islamic bomb. Allah, may peace be upon Him."

"Yeah, yeah. What else do you need?"

"That depends on the customer, but I would say eleven thousand centrifuges for uranium enrichment, for starters. I have a team of Germans and South Africans already working on that. They're very clever, the Germans. They are disguising the equipment as a water purification plant supposedly ordered by Jordan."

"Yeah, very clever. That's why they lost the war. Are the Jordanians in on this, too?"

"Just a couple of customs officials who have been well-paid to say the right thing. Now may I ask you a question, Mr. Cartwright?"

"Yeah, yeah, you can have another Scottish."

"Well, that wasn't it, but thank you, I will. No, my question is: Who is your bomb for?"

"Does it matter?"

"Not much. But I draw the line at the IRA."

"Why?"

"They made contact with me. A Mr. Joseph Cahill arranged through an intermediary to meet me in France, but then Mr. Cahill went to jail so they sent another person. A much younger man. He said his name was Billy."

Christ, Cartwright thought. Why send Billy? Why not McGuiness or McGuigan? "Mr. Khan, what did Billy want?"

"He only wanted a small bomb. One they could shoot out of a grenade launcher. I think they called it a dirty bomb. One that would contaminate a small area but terrify an entire population."

"Oh, so that's what they're up to. And what did you say?"

"I said I don't deal in such small matters. I was insulted."

"How much did he offer you?"

"Such a small amount. Only fifty thousand pounds."

Fifty thousand pounds! The money Gaddafi had been given that was stashed in the briefcase and dumped from the *Claudia.* Cartwright pondered. Did the Colonel know that was what had happened to his money? Jesus, the IRA was getting serious. And Billy was doing all their dirty work. Must have been him who'd killed the three Brits. And the IRA must've taken him in, right in. Malcolm would be pleased although he might be a bit nervous about facilitating an atomic weapon as well as a triple murder.

"Ayub, why don't you tell Mr. Khan about your boss's order?"

"My boss will give you all the yellowcake you want in exchange for a reactor and two warheads a month, plus a dummy reactor in another part of my country."

"And who is your boss, Mr. Ayub?"

"Colonel Muammar Gaddafi."

"Gaddafi!"

At this moment, Ayub chose to empty the money belt onto the bed. "That's a million pounds, Mr. Khan. It's yours. To show our good faith."

Khan trembled. "My god."

"No," Cartwright said, "our bomb. Now you have something to show us your goodwill?"

"Yes, yes. It's here in my briefcase. Plans for a sixteen-kiloton bomb."

"Oh, the ones you kept in the suitcase under your bed," Cartwright taunted.

"How did you know about that?"

"As I said, Mr. Khan, we are watching you very closely. We don't want to be double-crossed."

"Gentlemen, this cash assures you I will not."

"With the yellowcake, we reckon twenty mill should about do it."

"It should."

"We'll give you another ten million when the reactor is built, another five for the first bomb, and another five for the dummy plant. Plus all the yellowcake you need," Ayub said.

"Shut up," Cartwright suddenly whispered hoarsely. "Listen. There's somebody outside!" He whipped out his Glock, slipped off the safety catch, and took dead aim at the door. He raised a finger to his lips.

Ayub drew his gun and held it to Khan's head.

If this was a trap, it was a work of art. On the bed: a million pounds in cash. In the room: the CIA, a Libyan secret agent, and a thief of atomic secrets.

Cartwright's brain raced through the possibilities. *Who the hell would know about the meeting? Could be anyone. Who would want to stop the bomb-buying? Who would want to stop Gaddafi at all cost? It had to be the Israelis. If it is them, they'll have the attack well-planned. Two assassins, probably. First, they'll toss in a stun grenade, kill the Libyan and me, and haul Khan away. He's more valuable alive than dead. Us?*

He pretended not to notice that he couldn't keep his gun steady. Was this how it ended? In a shithole of a goddam hotel in fucking Holland?

Ayub and Bob stared at the door.

On Bob Cartwright's signal, Ayub swung his gun to the door while Bob screwed the silencer on his Glock.

Khan sat motionless. Terrified.

Tap. Tap. A soft knock.

Cartwright leaned into the peephole, but it was clear. They must be standing to the side. Using hand signals, he indicated that on the count of three, both he and Ayub would swing the door open, start firing, and kill the Mossad agents.

"One," Cartwright mouthed. "Two."

In slow motion, he reached for the handle and rested his grip on the knob.

"Three!"

Bam. Bam. Pht, Pht. Four shots.

We got the sons of bitches! Got them before they got us! Holy Jesus, that was close.

Except—when they opened the door and examined the bloodied corpses—they didn't see two Israeli assassins. Just two chambermaids who had, it appeared, come to turn down the beds.

"Jesus," Cartwright said. "We've just killed two women. Quick. Help me load them into their cart. We'll cover them with sheets and get the hell out of here."

The door to the next room opened.

"What's all the noise out here?" The inquirer was a young English women hotel guest, exquisitely dressed in a body-clinging blue gown that revealed her hard nipples and stunning body. She didn't appear to be wearing underwear. She oozed sex.

She looked down and saw the two bodies.

The scream was just forming at the back of her throat when Cartwright's bullet blew off half her head. They dumped her in the cart first, and then Ayub bent to pick up the first chambermaid.

He froze. The maid was a man! When he tugged at the head, the wig came away in his hands. Then he saw the Uzi submachine gun. "Mossad. I was right!"

Cartwright gasped. "Ayub! They'll have two more agents outside in a get-away car. Tie Khan up and blindfold him. Make it look like we were trying to kidnap him. I'll get the money and the blueprints. We've got three minutes before the other Israelis get here. I ran this drill with them in Langley. Three minutes!"

He faced Khan. "Khan! Listen! We're going to make it look like a kidnapping. Tell them you were invited here for dinner. You don't know who we were. Don't say a word about the plans or the syndicate. If anyone even gets a hint of it, you'll be dead, too. We'll contact you. Ayub! Let's go."

Cartwright and Ayub raced down the rear fire escape, sidled around to the front of the hotel, and hid behind the bushes. They would wait until the Israelis ran into the hotel and then take off.

Exactly three minutes after the shootings, they heard a car door slam and the hurried footsteps of the Mossad agents mounting the pathway to the hotel.

Cartwright could not see them clearly, but he did recognize the shape of an Uzi as the Israelis passed under the brightly lit hotel entrance.

"Okay. Let's go, Ayub."

They raced into the street and passed by a blue Volvo that Cartwright guessed was the Mossad car. He fired four bullets out of the silencer into its tires and sprinted to their rented van on which they had stuck Garden Supplies transparencies.

"Go! Go! Go!" Cartwright yelled to el-Sahafat.

The tires squealed when el-Sahafat gunned the accelerator.

"For Christ's sake, what are you doing? Are you trying to tell the fucking Mossad where we are? Take it easy! Now head up this street and take a right at the lights. That'll put us on the route to Germany. In ten minutes, when we're well clear, stop at the first phone booth."

"Kusemek,"[9] the first Mossad agent muttered.

"Kusemek," his partner echoed.

---

[9] Kusemek: Hebrew for "motherfucker." The Hebrew translates into "machood" in Urdu.

They'd shown false Dutch police passes to the young girl at the reception desk, who drew on her cigarette and nodded. Her name was Jock, an abbreviation for Jocasta.

In perfect Dutch, they had told her not to answer the phone or allow anyone to go to the second floor until they had finished. "We got a call from the other two policemen. They need help in questioning one of your guests, so we don't want to be interrupted."

After the two Mossad men left, she, not a fan of the police, had muttered: "Moederneukers."[10]

Upstairs, the Israelis had found Khan, bound and gagged, in his own shitload of trouble.

"What did the CIA want from you?" one of the Mossad men had asked, holding a handkerchief over his nose and mouth.

"They thought I could steal uranium from Urenco. I told them that was impossible. They tried to bribe me, but I said it's no use. Even if I wanted to, I couldn't because I do not have security clearance. Please, sir, may I have a Scottish?"

"There," Cartwright said. "On the right. There's a phone booth."

The Chief Petty Officer pulled over, and Cartwright made the call.

"British Airways travel assistance. How may I help you?"

"I've left my ticket at the Jachtlust Hotel in Almelo, Holland. I want it retrieved immediately."

"Is that just one ticket, sir?"

"There are a few others I left in the room. Two are still active, but three others have expired."

"What room should we go to?"

"Room two oh three on the second floor."

"Anything else you need to tell me?"

---

10 The mother of Oedipus, history's first true "moederneuker."

"Two of the tickets were for Tel Aviv, and I'm not sure where I left them exactly."

"And what is your account number, sir?"

"Zero five five two three eight."

"Thank you, sir. The matter will be attended to immediately."

"Yes, yes, please have a shower," one of the Mossad men said to Khan. "You smell like shit. Then we'll talk some more."

"We can take him with us," the other one said, "but we'll have to get rid of the bodies first."

The two Mossad men were undecided what to do about their dead colleagues and the girl.

"Shouldn't we take Zev and Avi back to Israel for burial?"

"Yes, but if we do that..." He never finished his sentence.

Four guns were aimed at their heads.

The shower must have covered the noise, for they never heard a thing.

Although Almelo is a small town, the Dutch police kept a unit of Special Forces on twenty-four-hour alert because of the Urenco facility. The message from MI6 was flashed to them within thirty seconds of Cartwright's call. They'd clambered up the back fire escape, silently edged along the dimly lit second floor, and passed the laundry box and its unwashed contents. They paused, heard the voices. Silly bastards had left the door open.

So much for the mystique of the mighty Mossad, handcuffed and hauled away.

Next, the shower. The Special Forces operatives wore night goggles, microphones, and black visors and were bestrewn with guns and daggers and grenades. One ripped back the shower curtain.

Khan screamed. "Who are you? What is going on?"

"We've just saved your life, Mr. Khan."

"How do you know who I am?"

"Oh, we were told to look out for a little Pakistani who works at Urenco. I can see you're a Pakistani, so you must be Khan. What happened here tonight?"

A.K. repeated his story about the bribery attempt, the kidnapping, and the Israelis. He was a simple scientist and knew nothing about bombs. They'd all made a very big mistake. He did not even have security clearance at Urenco.

London had told the Special Forces operators that if Khan was still alive to get him out of the way before the regular cops arrived.

That was the last the town of Almelo ever saw of A.K. Khan.

CHAPTER THIRTEEN

Late 1973

"So, Henry, this yellow cake stuff. What exactly is it?"

"It is uranium oxide, Mr. President. It's used in making nuclear fuel pellets essential for atomic bombs. But did you know yellowcake is not really yellow?"

"Why in the fuck call it yellow cake if it's not yellow, Henry?"

"It used to be yellow when it was first processed, but now new methods turn it black or gray."

"So why not call it black cake? Is this one of those stupid racial things? If it's black cake, let's call it fucking black cake."

"But then nobody would know what you're talking about, Mr. President, and that would be most unusual."

"Are you taking the piss out of the President of the United States, Henry? Because if you are, I'll fucking send you back to Hitlerland so fast your Kraut accent will get there ten hours before you do! Do I make myself clear, Henry?"

"You can't send me anywhere, Mr. President. I am a U.S. citizen, and perhaps you have forgotten I also have won the Nobel Peace Prize."

"What a fucking scam that was, Henry. You and that Viet Cong prick Le Fuck Sho. Still, you were generous to give into my demands for half the money. So, all right. Now, where were we?"

"Yellowcake, Mr. President. You wanted to know more about it."

"Where does it come from?"

"Canada, Australia, and Niger."

"Did you say 'Nigger,' Henry? I didn't think we were allowed to say that anymore."

"No, didn't say that. I said Niger. It's spelled N-i-g-e-r and pronounced 'neeg-air,' with a soft 'g.'"

"A soft 'g' as in Jesus Christ, not gorgonzola?"

"Exactly, Mr. President."

"And remind me, Henry, why I should give a flying fuck where it comes from?"

"Because Gaddafi can get his hands on a lot of it since Niger is right next door."

"And he's going to use it to trade with the Ugandans for their nuclear technology. I remember now."

"Almost, Mr. President. But not the Ugandans. They're in southern Africa and can't afford a box of matches let alone a nuclear reactor. No, if you remember, the CIA told us Libya was going to trade with Pakistan."

"The Pakis! Of course. That fucker in the loincloth Ali Butter. Knock, knock, Henry."

"I beg your pardon, Mr. President?"

"Knock, fucking, knock, Henry!"

"I'm sorry. Mr. President, I—"

"Knock, fucking, knock, Henry!"

"Oh, I see. Um. Who's there, Mr. President?"

"Ali."

"Ali who?"

"Al-I want for Christmas is my two front teeth! Ha, ha, ha. Gotcha, Henry."

"Yes, you did, Mr. President. Have you lost your teeth? They all seem to be in place."

"Listen, you stupid sausage-hugger, that's what we Americans call a joke. But you wouldn't know anything about that, being a fucking foreigner. Talking of foreigners, Schlesinger thinks we should bomb Libya just to let Gaddafi know we're onto him. And he says we could bomb Ireland and the Pakis at the same time."

"Which part of Ireland did he suggest we bomb?"

"He didn't care. I think he mentioned Brixton or Bristol, something that began with a 'B.'"

"Broadway?"

"Broadway? No that wasn't it. Shit, imagine if we dropped one on Broadway. They could—oh, Henry, ha, ha, they could, ha, ha, say the show bombed!"

"Yes, they could. But they won't because we are not going to. Didn't you write the name of the place down?"

"Never write anything down, Henry. Too many prying eyes around here. You never know who's a spy. No, I rely on my memory. Never fails, Henry."

"So we can bomb Brixton or Bristol, neither of which is in Ireland. And the British might be the tiniest bit offended, don't you think, Mr. President?"

"Jesus, you're right, Henry. Their prime minister, that pipe-smoking Scottish bastard Harold Wilson would go fucking berserk."

"Especially if you called him Scottish. He's English. Tell you what, Mr. President, why don't you sleep on it? We don't have to bomb anything tonight. I'll have a word with Schlesinger in the morning, and we can review his scenarios."

"Brussels? No. That's a vegetable. Bulgaria? No. Bagotville, Quebec? No. Bora Bora? No. Bhutan. No, that's a lighter. Bombay! Bombay! Bomb-fucking-bay! That's it."

"Is Bombay in Ireland, Mr. President?"

"Have you got a map, Henry? Doesn't matter. With a name like that, bomb and bay, it's a natural. Has to be in Ireland."

"I'll ask Seth to get the co-ordinates for Bombay, Ireland, although it may take him some time."

"Good work, Henry. See, never write anything down. Trust me."

"Well, Mr. President," Kissinger said, "it's been a long day, so I'll say arschloch."[11] *A long day, but a perfect short "goodnight."*

"Oh, thank you, Henry, and a good arschloch to you."

Arschloch. Ger.

[11] Translation from German: asshole.

CHAPTER FOURTEEN

The small flat on Romilly Road was cold. Night had fallen and along with it the temperature in the damp room. Mustaffa Fakih had been drawing information out of Mariam Hussein for the last hour.

"Mrs. Hussein, would you mind if I put a couple of shillings in the metre?"

"Oh, I'm sorry. I forgot how cold it gets in here. Would you like some more coffee, Mr. Fakih?"

"Yes, please, if it's not too much trouble. I've just got a couple of more questions, then I'll stop bothering you."

"It's no bother, Mr. Fakih. It's been helpful to be able to talk about it. What else do you want to know?"

"Did you come across any names in those documents you handed to the ambassador?"

"Um, I do remember one. It struck me as strange because it wasn't a Libyan name, or even Arabic. Just initials and a surname. But I remember thinking it was still a Muslim name."

"Do you remember the name now, Mrs. Hussein?"

Fakih knew if he got the name, the puzzle might, just might, start falling into some kind of order. And if he got the name, he would have a clue to a huge story. The Algerians and Libyans fighting over an atomic bomb? But how would Gaddafi get a bomb? He was giving away weapons to terror groups all over the world. So was it a quid pro quo? You give me a bomb and I give you—what the hell could Gaddafi give? Oil? Sure. Money? Sure. *But everyone's got plenty of both,* he thought. *What's he got the others don't?*

"Actually, Mr. Fakih, there is something I have not told you. I kept my own copies of those two documents. They are in Arabic."

"May I see them?"

"I suppose so. I have them hidden inside this candy from Brighton. Brighton rock.[12] It will take me a minute to get them out. It's a trick I learned in Algeria. Hollow out a sweet, insert the document, wrap it again. Pretend it's a souvenir and no one ever asks to eat it." After fumbling with the candy, she held out one of the papers. "Here."

Fakih took the letter-sized document, held it under the single bare lightbulb, and began to read:

> Great Socialist People's Libyan Arab Jamahiriya. Our great Revolutionary Leader, Col. Muammar Abu Minyar al-Qadhafi, has ordered that we and our Sunni brothers give praise to Allah, praise be upon His name, and honour Him with the greatest gift we know—the eternal preservation of our one true religion, Islam, and the annihilation of all others. Our great Revolutionary Leader understands we may be forced to engage in nefarious dealings with infidels and pay them large amounts of money. Allah will forgive us for it is His name that we must acquire the methods of mass destruction.

Fakih stared at the document, printed on official stationery. Was it a fake? Here was Gaddafi saying he was going to acquire atomic bombs and blow up "all others."

---

[12] A type of hard stick-shaped boiled sugar confectionery, usually flavoured with peppermint or spearmint, commonly sold at various tourist resorts, prefaced with the place of origin.

He studied the script again. It looked genuine. He stared up at Mariam Hussein and almost in a whisper asked, "Can I see the other document?"

She handed him the second sheet, which appeared to have been stapled to the first one but was now detached. The photocopier had been careful. Unlike the first document, this one was hand-written in pen and ink. It was brief and scratchy. Fakih strained to make out the words: Pakistan. Ready.

Underneath, in smaller, different writing, someone had appended a name. Fakih held it closer to the light. He could barely make it out.

"It's a name, isn't it, Mrs. Hussein? Do you know what it says?"

"The name is A.K. Khan."

"So do I take it that A.K. Khan is a Pakistani scientist who will help Gaddafi?"

"Exactly, Mr. Fakih. The Algerians traced Mr. Khan to a nuclear facility in Holland, but now he's disappeared. But he's the man. All we have to do is find him."

"And your husband's body. Mrs. Hussein, may I borrow these documents? I'll make my own photocopies and bring them back to you tomorrow."

"Um, I'm not sure about that Mr. Fakih. I—"

"I know it's getting late, but would you come with me to my office while I do it? Then I can give them straight back to you. Mrs. Hussein, this is material you cannot use except as a spy. I can use it as a journalist. They suspected your husband and killed him. If anyone gets the idea that you are an Algerian agent, which you are now, then they, whoever they are, will not hesitate to kill you."

"But so far, no one has any reason to suspect I know anything."

"Mrs. Hussein, we're talking about atomic bombs and Gaddafi blowing up half the world!"

"No. no. It's all right, Mr. Fakih. What you say is right. But please bring them back tomorrow."

"Is there a back way out of your house?" Fakih suddenly felt vulnerable and even a little scared.

“No, there is not, but the front is not well-lit, so it would be hard to see anyone leaving this place.”

“Can you tell if you’re still being watched?”

“I can’t. It’s too dark. But just in case, do what I do. Go straight to Finsbury Park tube station and get on the first train that comes along. It doesn’t matter where it’s going. Then, after two stops, get off the train at the last second. Get on the next one just before the doors close. That should shake any person following you. Then change again after a couple of stops and go to your real destination. But please be careful, Mr. Fakih. As you said to me, we are dealing with killers who want an atomic bomb. The stakes do not get much higher than that.”

CHAPTER FIFTEEN

November 17, 1974

"Now on BBC One, the Nine O'clock News, with Robert Dougall."

"Good evening. The President of the United States Richard Nixon has resigned."

Malcolm Forbes-Smythe had his Temeraire bedecked with three TV sets all parroting the same story. But he barely looked up as Dougall, Britain's famous bird-watching newsreader, intoned an introduction to Nixon lying to the world: "I am not a crook."

"No, and I'm not the Queen of England." Forbes-Smythe muttered the half-truth so his guests could not quite hear him. His guests were transfixed, not by the Watergate saga but by what Forbes-Smythe had just told them.

His agents had killed the wrong person in Finsbury Park's lovely green spaces. Not that it mattered. The chauffeur's body would be cleaned up and delivered to his grieving widow the following morning. But their special communications people had picked up an interesting phone call. The translation indicated the Algerian Embassy in

London was going to interfere with Gaddafi's special delivery. They had received information from a driver's wife, who had named the person who would help them.

Cartwright was the first to react. "His wife? He was feeding her information? She's the spy?"

"We checked on Mariam Hussein and found that she was in the FLN as a kid. She was jailed and tortured by the French. Getting Gaddafi's bomb would be the perfect way to give Algeria the kudos it so badly wants but can't afford. And it would scare the French very badly. A rather nice 'touché,' don't you think?"

"But, Malcolm, are you going to let her? She could really fuck up our plans."

"And what about my money?" A.K. Khan asked.

Khan, along with Bob Cartwright and Ayub el-Sahafat, had been whisked to a small airfield in Holland where an unmarked private jet, whose registration number was changed every few days, had flown to a landing strip outside London.

"No, Bob, she will not interfere with our plans. When the undertakers deliver her Yuseff's body tomorrow, they'll discover to their horror that she has died of an accidental overdose of gas from her heater. Happens all the time. The flames go out, but the gas keeps on coming. Our boys are rigging it up now. I'm told a nosy journalist delayed us by a few minutes, but he's gone now. Both corpses will be delivered to the Algerian Embassy. I think they'll get the message, don't you?"

"Isn't this going too far, Malcolm? So far we've got seven dead British soldiers, two dead Mossad, and one tourist. Now two Algerians. That's twelve." Ayub could cold-count the dead as easily as the millions of dollars that would miraculously transcend him from Islam to a Buddhist Nirvana that only money could buy.

"Oh well," Bob countered.

"Listen," Malcolm said, "we are dealing with nuclear bombs here. Nuclear bombs that will be detonated by madmen. Ever thought how many they might kill, Bob? Ten thousand? A hundred thousand? A couple of million? They could even set off a nuclear chain reaction and then we'd all be gone. The whole fucking planet. If twelve people get in the way, they're paying a very small price."

Just as Forbes-Smythe was finishing his diatribe, Tommy Beecham handed him a telex. "This just came in from the ops room."

"Anything you can share, Malcolm?" Cartwright inquired.

"Belfast. The Protestants have just blown up a Catholic pub. Full of IRA from all over the north. Our people reckon sixty dead."

"Sixty?" Cartwright raised his eyebrows.

"Sixty. That'll wipe out most of the active IRA forces in Belfast."

"But isn't that good news? They wiped out your competition with just one bomb."

"No, it's the worst possible news," Forbes-Smythe said. "The Protestants will think they've won. Crippled the IRA. But all they've done is assured that more boyos from the south will now join up and want revenge. God knows what they'll do to get even. That bomb tonight will mean Downing Street will want answers. How come we didn't know? We've got thirty SAS men on the ground and we didn't know! What are we doing about it? How can we stop the Provos from hitting back? How do we stop those idiotic Prods from doing it again? They'll be on a high. Watch for the riots tomorrow. As much as I despise them, no Catholic is safe. That means we are not safe here, either. If I were the IRA, I would hit London with everything I've got. But if we act quickly, we might be able to scare the shit out of the Prods and assuage the IRA at the same time." Forbes-Smythe stopped. He'd just remembered. "Billy! The message didn't mention Billy, did it, Tommy?"

"No, Malcolm."

"When will we know?"

"It was a thousand-pound bomb in a petrol tanker that rammed the pub. The damage would have been terrible. It could take days to identify all the bodies," Tommy replied.

"So how do they know there were sixty dead?"

"Just an educated guess. You go to bomb blasts often enough you get pretty good at estimating the dead and wounded."

"So no word about Billy?"

"No. But if the top leadership was there, it's a good guess it was Billy."

"Are we sure it was the Prods, Tommy?"

"It could have been the IRA themselves, provoking just the kind of reaction you're talking about. It could have been Belfast cops' special ops trying to end the IRA trouble once and for all. But my guess is that it was the UVF."

"UVF?" Cartwright interjected.

"The Prod paras, known as the Ulster Volunteer Force," Tommy replied.

Forbes-Smythe glanced at a movement at the doorway. It was Khan, back sooner than he'd expected. He had been feeling quite ill and had gone for a nap. He'd also been sweating like a, well, goat. Sweating like a pig would have been embarrassing even to a bad Muslim. And he needed to change his very wet, febrile-flooded attire.

"Ah, Mr. Khan, feel better now? That Chinese silk dressing gown is rather fetching despite your hirsute legs. Would you like a drink? I thought so. Now, Mr. Khan, you were rather disparaging when your IRA contact mentioned a dirty bomb. You said fifty thousand pounds wasn't enough and you don't deal with such trivialities."

"That is true. I am a nuclear scientist, not a fire-cracker maker."

"Yes. Yes. But the thing is, old chum, I want you to make such a bomb, and I want it now."

"Mr. Malcolm, I will not do this. It is beneath a man of my talents."

"Would a man of your talents like to be delivered to the Algerian Embassy tomorrow morning in a coffin just like two others who are on that very same delivery route?"

"You wouldn't dare, Mr. Malcolm. Without me, you have no real bomb."

"Bob, I believe you have a little speciality that could persuade Mr. Khan."

Cartwright jumped to his feet, brushed the glass out of Khan's hand, and clamped on the man's carotid sinus nerve.

Khan's choking body slumped to the carpet.

"Now let me tell you what I want, Mr. Khan. I want you to make the IRA their dirty bomb. Only cut the radiation component by ten. That means they and the UVF will think they have a weapon that will cause radiation and possible death over a small area for about a year. But we know Semtex will make it go 'bang' and perhaps cause a little radiation poisoning, some vomiting, loss of hair, that sort of thing. Just enough to terrify the Prods into not doing a pub bomb again. We'll let our chaps tell the UVF that the IRA has an unlimited supply, so they'd better knock it off. Okay?"

Khan looked up from the floor. "How much will you pay me?"

"We'll supply the materials. The uranium, the rocket launcher. Range anywhere from three hundred yards to eight miles. And we've got a couple almost ready to be assembled. Oh, fifty thousand does sound about right? Excellent. We have a private facility where no one will disturb you or ask any tricky questions."

***

Fakih had set his alarm for 7:00 a.m., but he was out of bed by six, nervous and troubled by the prior night's events. His apartment, just off Sloane Square, was an immaculate hand-me-down from the previous *Al-Ahram* representative who believed that foreign correspondents were a rarefied breed who should live like his country's most senior diplomats. But Fakih drew the line at chauffeurs and maids, though he did have a Portuguese woman come in twice a week to clean and wash up after him.

At seven, the alarm went off. Damn! He'd forgotten to turn it off. *No, that's not the alarm, it's the phone.*

"Hello, Fakih here," he said in Arabic, thinking it might be his editors in Cairo.

"Hello, is that Mr. Fakih?"

"Oh. Oh, yes. Sorry, I thought you were Cairo."

"No. That's all right, Mr. Fakih. Mr. Fakih this is... Well, let's just say for the moment that I am a friend with a message."

Fakih began taking notes furiously.

"Mr. Fakih, I believe you were going to visit Mrs. Hussein on Romilly Road this morning?"

"How did you know that? Who are you?"

"All in good time, Mr. Fakih. The thing is, you shouldn't go to Romilly Road this morning."

"Why not?"

"You don't want to get tied up in a police investigation, do you?"

"What police investigation?"

"Oh, I'm so sorry. You haven't heard, have you?"

"Heard what, for god's sake?" Fakih's voice was rising in anger and fear at the casual, almost lazy voice on the other end of the phone.

"At about four o'clock this morning, a police constable, just out of police college, a real keener if you know what I mean—"

"Yes. Yes," Fakih interrupted impatiently.

"Well, this constable was doing his rounds, and he came to Romilly Road. He thought he smelled gas coming from one of the houses. The young lad kept his wits about him. Didn't break the door down or anything like that. Cool as a cucumber he was."

"What happened?" Fakih was almost yelling.

"I'm getting to that, Mr. Fakih. He radioed his duty sarge, who called the fire brigade. They got there lickety-split, put on their breathing gear, and went in. And that's when they found Mrs. Hussein."

"Where?"

"Slumped in a chair. It seems the gas flame had blown out, but the gas just kept on coming. She wouldn't have felt anything. She would have just gone to sleep."

"You mean she's dead?"

"I'm very sorry, sir, but yes. They reckon she passed away about ten last night."

"But I left her not long before nine."

"Perhaps the breeze from the door blew the flame out. But don't blame yourself, sir. It was an accident. The police won't bother you, sir. They have all the necessary facts."

"How do you know? And you still haven't told me who you are."

"Oh, you can call me Tommy, sir. And let's just say I work for the government."

"What part of government?"

"Never mind that, Mr. Fakih. But I think you should meet my boss and me. For your own good, if you know what I mean."

"My own good? Am I in danger?"

"Could be, sir. We'd like you to meet us for lunch today."

"I'm sorry, Mr. Tommy, but I already have a lunch engagement with, how shall I put it? A lady friend."

"Cancel it, sir. Meet us at the Churchill Hotel at twelve-thirty. You know it? In Portman Square. Ask for the party booked under the name of Delius. Got that?"

"Delius?"

"Yes, as in the composer. And bring that book by Graham Greene."

"What book?"

"Oh, Mr. Fakih, don't disappoint me. He's one of our most famous writers. Don't tell you've never read him."

"Of course, I have. *The End of the Affair, The Quiet American, The Heart of The Matter*."

"No. None of those. Mr. Fakih, bring the book. The one written in 1938."

"*Brighton Rock*?"

"Yes. That special edition you borrowed from Mrs. Hussein."

***

A.K. Khan took his umbrage to the farthest corner of Malcolm's Temeraire. He had never been so insulted. Ordered by the bloody British to make a puny dirty bomb.

He was a master. A true maestro of the world's greatest nuclear orchestra. His multi-national creations would be works of genius that only he could compose. The wealth would make him the most revered man in Pakistan. And the Irish wanted a dirty bomb.

Let's see how dirty I can make it, he mused. *They'll never know. That's the beauty of nuclear science. And I've constructed a revolutionary protective shield so powerful and yet so thin, no one handling it will be contaminated. Virtually nobody knows anything about such genius. The IRA will be in for a surprise when they fire this beauty. And so will the poor fools on the other side.*

"Mr. Malcolm, I think it is ready."

"Do you need to test it somehow?"

"Oh, no. That would not be a good idea. When we fire this one, it will go off for real. I am sure of that."

"Okay, A.K. Ha, ha. Now we have to arrange delivery. Do they need any special instructions?" Forbes-Smythe asked.

"No. Mr. Malcolm, this is a beautiful, simple little device. All they have to do is load it into one of their grenade launchers and pull the trigger. Poof! I've built this one to explode after it has gone one thousand metres. That means the terrorists can choose, say, a nice high building with a clear view of their target, and let it go."

"But you've used only a tiny amount of actual uranium, right, Mr. Khan?

"Of course, sir, that was the deal. I had one of your scientists check it himself."

Khan failed to mention he had paid the scientist twenty thousand pounds to verify the fake load.

***

When the head of the Royal Ulster Constabulary called in Jimmy Crozier to tell him about the IRA's new weapon, the UVF boss thought his old friend was kidding. They'd chosen a memory lane of horror for their stunning message—the infamous RUC Castlereagh interrogation centre.

"Jaysus, Tom. You're pulling my dick, so you are?"

"No, Jimmy. They've got one, and the next time you blow them up, we won't be able to protect you against a nuclear weapon."

"Jaysus. When yoos says it like that, nookulah weapon, that's fookin' serious. So it is."

"So tell your lads to stop right now. Don't provoke them anymore. We'll try to intercept their new toy, but I'm getting very mixed signals from the Brits."

"What could this nookulah weapon do, Tom?"

"Kill half of fucking Belfast. Your half, Jimmy, and cause cancer for generations."

"Jaysus fookin' Chroist. Where'd they get it?"

"Oh, no doubt Cahill did some kind of deal with Gaddafi. The Garda might have missed it on the *Claudia* or handed it straight over to the IRA. I don't know, really. But mark my words, Jimmy, they've got it, and as we know, those mad bastards will use it. Don't give them an excuse."

"If you grab it from them, will yoos give it to us, Tom?"

"Could do, Jimmy."

***

"Malcolm," Tommy said, "you're not going to believe this. Billy was not in the pub when it blew up. He was in Londonderry giving instructions to the local battalion commander, Martin McGuiness."

"He was giving instructions to McGuiness? Are you sure it wasn't the other way round?" Malcolm Forbes-Smythe asked.

"No. Billy has made quite a name for himself after killing our three men. Cahill heard of it from prison and has put the word out that Billy is to take over special assignments. He's worried McGuigan will crack if he's picked up so he wants to groom a successor."

"It's going better than we hoped, Tommy. I think we should find out what he can do with Mr. Khan's dirty bomb. That would, as it were, rocket him to the top of the IRA in a great hurry. And while we're at it, let's use el-Sahafat to arrange the consignment. He's an expert in getting things in and out of Northern Ireland. If he gets caught, then we're in the clear. I'm sure he can hire a fishing boat on the British coast. He's a certified sea captain, so he should be able to find the drop-off point our lads arrange with Billy."

"Of course, Bob will have to go with him," Tommy said. "I still don't trust Ayub, Malcolm. Or Khan, for that matter."

"Of course. Why don't we get Mr. Khan to go along, too? Just to take care of the consignment. We don't want it going off in British waters."

"Ah, that might not be a very good idea, Malcolm. I hear Mr. Khan gets very seasick."

"Precisely, Tommy. Precisely."

***

A.K. Khan paled at the news. He'd rigged the bomb to blow a large portion of Belfast, and he was going to be in full vomit mode for as many as three days. He was a most unhappy world's greatest nuclear scientist. But, by now, he knew not to protest. That headlock or a gunshot to the head would soon change his mind. He knew the British were ruthless, but he had never seen this side of them, although it didn't bother him that he was building weapons of mass destruction that could wipe out an entire country. And with the promise of hundreds of millions of dollars, what was a genius to do?

The Divis Flats was an instant 1966 concrete ghetto filled with indigent Catholic families and the scene of many battles. At the bottom of the Catholic Falls Road, they also abutted the Protestant enclave that included the infamous Shankill Road, which was ablaze in taunting murals of King William of Orange and his victory of the Catholics three centuries previously, the ubiquitous "Fuck the Pope" graffiti, Union Jacks both painted and flying, defiant murals of the masked men of the UVF and UDA. And how did the Catholics feel?

The Republican publication *The Starry Plough,* eulogizing one death in the Divis Flats, wrote:

> He was only nine, when Patrick Rooney, also aged nine, was shot dead in his bedroom in Divis Flats by those same licensed murderers, leading the loyalist pogroms as they sprayed the people's homes with Browning machine gunfire from their Shoreland armoured car.

Or, to put it in Yeats's language, they were highly pissed off. No terrible beauty had been born here. No falconer heard the falcon. Just guns, living in fear, and death and hatred.

***

"What a splendid place to launch Mr. Khan's device. The locals will give the IRA cover. From the roof, all they have to do is take quick aim, at which I'm told they are rather excellent, and pull the trigger. Champers all 'round?"

Malcolm Forbes-Smythe was in very high spirits. The drop off the coast of Ireland had gone perfectly. Khan had puked all the way. Downing Street was not too anxious about the pub bomb when Malcolm told the PM of his plan. Harold Wilson was sick to his teeth with the fucking Irish problem. This might make it all go away. And it almost did.

***

Billy and Bernie, the small wiry grenade man from County Cork, clambered up the twelve flights of stairs to the roof of the flats. They gasped for air as their three armed escorts followed. It had just gone six in the evening, and the locals were all indoors, watching themselves riot on the BBC News.

"Keep down now, lads," Billy directed, "until we're ready. We don't want any British bastards to spot us. Here, drape the camouflage over us in case their fucking chopper flies over. Bernie, will you be able to get up, take aim, and fire before anyone sees you?"

"Oh, to be sure, Billy, that I can. You just tell me when."

"So aim just over the Shankill. Should scare the bejeezus out of the prods all eating their fucking dinners."

"And this is just a small explosion with a bit of nuclear fallout?" Bernie enquired.

"The Semtex will make one fucking great bang and flatten a few houses, but it's the radioactivity that'll scare the shit out of them. There's only a drop of it in the bomb, but the UVF have been told it's the real thing. Could kill thousands, they've been told. This'll stop the fuckers from blowing any more of our lads. Just watch. Are you ready, Bernie?"

"Aye, Billy. I'm ready. Just let me check on the wind. Light coming from behind us. Perfect."

The men on the roof fell silent as Bernie twisted himself into firing position, hoisted the loaded launcher on his right shoulder, peered through the sights, made a tiny adjustment, and pulled the trigger. The blast blew him five feet backwards, and he crashed into the four men under the camouflage.

"Jeezus! What the fuck was that?" he screamed.

"Fuck me, lads! Let's get the fuck out of here now!"

Nobody argued. They'd never seen a rocket go off like that.

Bernie grabbed the launcher and began sprinting down the stairs. *Fuck! What was that?*

"Fuck. What was that?" were the last words ever uttered by Ian Roscommon and a hundred and fifty others in the Shankill that night. Houses collapsed, crushing entire families. Gas mains burst, and flames turned the tinderbox row houses into deathtraps. Cars blew up, petrol stations exploded, and animals on the street were incinerated.

Then the deadly rumours began. A nuclear bomb. Ambulance staff in full protective gear added to the panic. Screaming, hysterical Protestants sprinted away from the catastrophe. First in the tens, then in the hundreds. Within ten minutes, the streets of Belfast were jammed with terrified death-stricken victims.

Police tried to herd the mobs down streets away from the explosion, but most cops simply fled. They didn't want to die the death of radiation poisoning or cancer, either. The TV stations went silent. The BBC put up a notice saying that due to an extreme incident, all programmes were suspended.

A rumour swept through the stampeding crowd that the Europa Hotel, a few minutes from the epicentre, had a bomb shelter. It didn't. But the mobs hacked and killed guests, journalists, bartenders, army officers. Anyone in their way.

Half an hour after Bernie pulled the trigger, at least a thousand were dead: killed by the bomb, trodden to death, or hacked to pieces by a wild, terrified populace wanting a frenzied revenge of a kind Northern Ireland had never seen.

At Lisburn Army Headquarters, they got their first radiation reading. "It says X 10 GY. That is extremely high. But there is good news. The wind is blowing it up into the atmosphere."

"Projections, Colonel?"

"Without the wind, I would say a ninety percent death rate. And then there would be the cancers and the gastrointestinal and bone marrow failures."

"So we could be looking at a hundred thousand dead?"

"That's a very rough estimate, General Jackson, sir, and includes all the civilian casualties caused by the rioting and killing on in the streets right now. But a lot depends on the wind."

"So what do we do?"

"We have to calm it, General, and very quickly. We also have to get in radiation specialists, contamination-proof wards, sterile gear, and oh yes, capture the bastards who did this."

"Commander, do we have any nuclear-proofed tanks here?"

"I believe the nearest are in Germany, sir."

"Get on to the Americans. Tell them what's up. I want those tanks on the streets of Belfast by morning. In the meantime, get our lads into the streets. Swamp the safe areas. Keep the rioters out at all costs. Otherwise, the entire city could blow. Any news from London?"

"They're trying to contact Mr. Wilson. Downing Street wants him to go on national TV. Calm the people. Assure them it was one isolated incident by one madman."

"But we don't know that."

"He can hardly say the IRA have just murdered maybe a hundred thousand of their countrymen, can he? The war would have only just begun."

"But wasn't there a whisper of a dirty bomb some time back?"

"There was, sir."

"Gaddafi?"

"We think so, but we aren't completely sure. Oh, by the way, sir, we'll have to put out a press statement right away and you should go on TV, too. We've already had a hundred requests."

"Okay, Lieutenant. Arrange the presser for twenty-two hundred hours here tonight."

"Sir!"

***

Malcolm Forbes-Smythe had not heard the news yet. He raised a Waterford crystal glass of Black Bushmills Irish whiskey to his lover, Jeremy. "It's a festive Irish night tonight, my pet, so I thought we'd honour the wee faeries across the water just this once."

"Something special in your silly spy business?"

Jeremy was a defrocked Catholic priest who had been caught with a seminarian. His sin was that he got caught, refused to service the bishop, and was excommunicated. He now ran an upscale men's clothing store on Bond Street. Malcolm suspected it was financed with hush money from the church for something Jeremy knew about the Cardinal.

They were sipping the "nectar of the Antrim" and were about to top up their glasses when the phone rang.

Malcolm picked up the receiver. "Tommy? The radio? Why not the TV? All right. All right. The radio. I'll call you back."

He replaced the receiver and walked towards the radio and turned it on.

"Don't tell me," Jeremy lightly barbed, "they playing your favourite song."

"Shut up. Listen."

> "...and early reports say there is bloody rioting on the streets in the centre of the city. We repeat: there is no confirmation yet that a nuclear device has been exploded; however, police are saying the death toll has already reached one thousand. Entire blocks of the Protestant Shankill Road section are on fire, and residents are pouring into hospitals demanding treatment for radiation poisoning. We're going live now to Belfast where the chief of defence forces, General Mike Jackson, has just started a news conference."

Even Jeremy gulped down another Black Bush. Uninterested, suave, debonair Jeremy prided himself in not giving a flying fuck about the quotidian bilge known as news. But not this day.

> "First, I'd like to make a statement, and then I'll take your questions. What we know so far is that at approximately six oh five tonight a device was fired from the Divis Street Flats area and exploded over the Shankill Road. The initial explosion caused the collapse of many houses and set off a large number of fires. About the rumours of a nuclear device being used, I shall be frank with you. Our intelligence unit had word that the IRA had acquired some form of low-level nuclear weapon and was preparing to use it in retaliation for the bombing of the pub in which sixty of them died. Do not panic when you hear this next piece of information, please. You are all relatively safe. But early readings in the atmosphere around the Crumlin

and Shankill Road areas do, indeed, indicate that a nuclear device was detonated. Its magnitude was much greater than we had been led to believe. But with favourable winds, most of the radiation will dissipate into the atmosphere and the danger will quickly pass. In the meantime, we are setting up camps to the south of the city, away from any possible contamination. You are all invited to sleep there, but a warning. We will not tolerate any further outbreaks of violence or any attempt to engage any community in reprisals. My men have orders to shoot to kill. We will not allow this province to be destroyed by one madman. By morning, you will see American battle tanks on your streets. They are specially designed for nuclear warfare. They will patrol any contaminated areas still remaining, and they will not hesitate to open fire on subversives."

"Another Irish, pet?" Jeremy was genuinely concerned.

"That fucking Khan. That fucking lying bastard. He double-crossed us."

Forbes-Smythe took the drink, downed it, picked up the phone. "Tommy. Twenty minutes. You know whom I wish to see. And Bob and el-Sahafat. Oh, and the Chief Superintendent."

***

"Mr. Khan. How nice to see you," a jovial Forbes-Smythe said. "I hope we didn't disturb you from anything important at this late hour."

"No, that's quite all right." Khan was bemused. He had no idea why he'd be called into MI6 so late at night.

"You're a cricket fan. Have you been following the Test match at the Oval? Your chaps are doing very well against England."

"Yes, but your Mr. Amiss scored a beautiful one eighty-three."

"He did indeed, but do you know who impressed me most today? Your bowler, Alam Intikhab. Five wickets for a hundred and sixteen runs. That is great bowling. Do you know anything about cricket, Bob?"

"I've seen a bit. Doesn't make any sense to me."

"Ayub?"

"I know a bit, Malcolm, but not as much as you and Mr. Khan."

"Are you a fan, Chief Superintendent?"

"Oh. Very big, sir. I agree. That Intikhab is some bowler."

"Tell you what, Superintendent, shall we show Bob and Ayub some of the finer points of the game, with Mr. Khan's help?"

Khan began to feel sick. He knew no good was to come of this. But why? "Mr. Malcolm, is anything wrong? Did anything happen today?"

"Ah, so that's why you're so relaxed. You haven't heard, have you?"

"Heard what?"

"Your bomb went off today. And it has killed a lot of people. I told you to make it very small. You disobeyed my orders. Now, cricket, anyone? Mr. Khan, would you kindly strip to your underwear."

"No. I will not."

"Bob?"

"Okay. Okay."

"Tommy, our floor is sealed off, and there's no access in or out, right?"

"Right, sir."

Malcolm went to a drawer in his desk and pulled out a shiny red cricket ball. "Souvenir from the old days. But it's the same as them all. It's made of cork, weighs about five ounces, and is hard as a rock. The bowler gets six attempts to get the batsman out and then another bowler has a turn. Let's go into the corridor where there's more room and I can show you the various ways to bowl a cricket ball. Mr. Khan, you'll be the batsman. Normally, behind you, we would have three wooden stumps, twenty-eight inches high. But as we don't have any stumps, I'll just have to aim for Mr. Khan's balls. He would also normally have a bat, but not tonight. Now, if he moves before I bowl, he's out, so then, Bob, you can take over."

"But, Mr. Malcolm, please do not do this. I am very sorry."

"And so are the thousand or so dead people. First, Initkhab's speciality, called a googly, where the ball bounces one way and then back the other. Very tricky."

Forbes-Smythe did a little skip as he trotted four or five paces and twisted his wrist as he let the ball go. It bounced in front of Khan, who tried to swat it away with his hands, but it bounced back the other way, just as advertised, and stung him viciously on the shins.

"Now, for a change, this one is called a fastball. Just like in your baseball, Bob. Can reach speeds of up to ninety miles an hour, though it'll be short of that since I don't have a long enough run-up. Ready, Mr. Khan?"

"Please stop. Please."

"Not a chance, old son. These gents have paid perfectly good money to see how the game is played. Here we go."

Forbes-Smythe, at the very end of the corridor now, turned and ran as fast as he could for ten yards and then let the ball fly. It bounced about five yards in front of Khan and crashed into his testicles.

Khan fell to the ground, writhing.

"Next, the full toss."

"Jesus, Malcolm, you sadist," Bob said. "Don't you think he's had enough?"

"Going soft on me, Bob? You of all people. Get him to his feet. Gentlemen, I give you the full toss. As its name suggests, the bowler pitches the ball higher this time so it does not bounce, but if given just the right trajectory, screams down onto the stumps. In this case, Khan's hip."

Khan fell to the ground again, screaming in pain.

"Two more to go, and then it's what we call 'over.'"

No one bothered to stop Forbes-Smythe.

"And now for your delectation, the body liner."

"Oh Jesus," the Chief Superintendent muttered.

Malcolm turned again, his long hair covered in sweat as it flopped over his forehead. In an almost-throwing motion, he hurled the ball at Khan. It bounced hard and flew straight into his face. Blood poured from his nose and mouth.

"Sir, I think that ought to do it. We don't want to have to take him to the hospital. Right now, we've got more work to do."

"You're right, Tommy. Okay, A.K., any more plans to double-cross me?"

"You bastard. I'll get you for this."

"No, you won't, old boy. You are too greedy. Now go and clean yourself up before a visitor arrives."

***

Chief Superintendent Bill Playter had been acting in a liaison role at MI6 for five years. Reliable, loyal, and corrupt. Just what Malcolm wanted. So, from the deck of his "fighting" Temeraire, Malcolm eschewed flag signals and picked up a device he called the telephone.

"Bill, you've found the name of the scientist who signed the false paperwork for Khan?"

"Yes, we have. He's well-known in his profession. Dr. Miles Baker. He lives in a posh house in Highgate. Pillar of society. Wife's a doctor. He's up for a knighthood, I'm told. And one other thing: one of my lads took a quick look at his bank records. The day the signature was dated, twenty thousand quid went into his account."

"Bill, how long would it take your lads to launch a full-scale night drug raid? Big lights, lots of marked cars, sirens, the lot."

"Half an hour."

"And what could you find?"

"First," Playter said, "we'd probably need a tip that he's transporting cocaine in his car doors. We can phone that in any time. That gives us an excuse to tear his house apart. And, of course, we'd find more cocaine."

"No way it's not his?"

"Not as far as any judges I know are concerned. They'll all play along. Anyhow, before it comes to trial he'll be ruined. We can go that route, or we can charge him with aiding and abetting nuclear proliferation, which would get him a solid twenty years. But then you'd have to give up some evidence and I gather that's not the plan."

"No. Let's do the drug raid. Tonight, Bill. And then bring him to me."

"Good as done, sir."

***

The morning papers did a great rush job:

> WHAT'S UP YOUR NOSE, DOC? BABY. HEAVY TRAFFIC IN HIGHGATE HIDEAWAY. DOC-A-BYE, BABY.

***

Of course, Dr. Miles Baker was still furious when he reached the Vauxhall Bridge headquarters of MI6 the next day. In one of his many hours of need, Malcolm summoned his unelected cabinet to do their duties—knee-scraping sycophants to fulfill critical duties of state, such as pouring an Irish or two. Superintendent Playter's task was to polish the Waterford crystal glasses, Ayub to fill them, and A.K Khan to drain the bottoms. Tom Beecham conducted the entire symphony in the manner of Delius.

Malcolm drew the lawyer aside. The conversation took five minutes.

The lawyer excused himself and informed Dr. Baker he could be of no further use. But he advised him to plead guilty to the drug charges or much worse would happen.

"I'll do no such thing. The whole thing's a bloody setup. You have no right whatsoever to disgrace me and my family with this grotesque series of lies. I'll sue you, the government, and the police for millions. I'm a respected scientist with friends in high places, I'll have you know."

"Not anymore you don't, Doctor," Malcolm said. "Or should I just call you Miles?"

"Please address me as Dr. Baker."

"Okay, Miles, have it your way. So, Miles, you've been a very bad lad, and you almost upset one of my most spectacular and important plans ever. And all for twenty thousand pounds."

"I don't know what you're talking about. I've never taken money from anyone in my life."

"So now you are lying. Oh dear, Miles, I wish you hadn't done that. Superintendent, if a house has been found to have been used for the trafficking of cocaine, what happens to it?"

"My house? You can't touch my house."

"Oh, I think the Superintendent's men and women did an excellent job with your house and your car last night. The repair bill will be enormous."

Baker's face went white. "And you'll pay every penny."

"No," Malcolm said. "You've been charged with a very serious offence. You refuse to cooperate. You have committed a crime against humanity—yes, that little thing with the bomb—so we need to teach you some more lessons. You've gone very quiet, Miles. Anything wrong?"

"I have nothing more to say."

"Let me do the talking for you. The Superintendent will help. Oh, by the way, have you seen Mr. Khan recently? Tommy, bring Mr. Khan in. Perhaps they'd like to share a cuppa?"

Khan hobbled into the room, barely able to sit, stand, or walk.

The bad doctor squeaked: "My god, A.K. What did they do to you?"

"Oh, we had a little game of cricket, that's all. They got you, too."

"For Christ's sake, shut up, A.K," an ashen Miles hissed.

"Sorry, Miles, but they know everything."

"Indeed we do," Forbes-Smythe interrupted. "Like the assessed value of your Highgate house, Miles. One point five million pounds. Mortgage, seven hundred fifty thousand pounds. But now that it's a known drug house, we estimate it will go for one hundred fifty thousand, so you'd be out over half a million quid."

"But I'm not selling it."

"Oh, sorry. I have papers here in your handwriting instructing it to go on the market immediately for one hundred fifty-nine thousand pounds."

"That's a lie! That's not my writing!"

"Our experts say it is. The house is already on the market. There's an open house tonight."

"You bastards!"

"Oh, that will be extra. We charge extra for bastards. Has your wife called you about the money she's been accused of stealing by overcharging the National Health by two million pounds? No? And has your son called to say he's been expelled from university for plagiarism? No? Now be a good boy, Miles, and get the fuck out of here. You are ruined. And you are going to jail. You wanted to say something, A.K.? No. Good. Very good."

CHAPTER SIXTEEN

Mustaffa Fakih decided to walk the two kilometres to the bookshop at the west end of King's Road. The morning was overcast but dry, and he still had over an hour and a half before his lunch date at the Churchill Hotel. He would call Cairo at five o'clock that evening. All he would tell his foreign editor was that he was onto a very big story but did not want to discuss it on the phone. Before that, he would telex a coded message about his lunch meeting and the probability of flying back to Cairo.

He thought about going to the Algerian Embassy to inquire after Mariam and Yuseff Hussein. Fakih was genuinely saddened and shocked at the news of her death although he had no time for spies or their creepy world. But Mariam had been dealt a bad hand in life—and in death, and Fakih wanted to acknowledge that. He wanted to grieve for her. No one else would. What about the kids, though? Who was going to tell them both their parents were dead?

Deep in thought, he almost walked straight past the Worlds End Bookshop.

An exquisite English "bit of crumpet"[13] wearing the world's shortest mini-skirt was descending a ladder when he entered the shop. She caught him as he gazed first at her long sensuous legs, moved up to her thighs, and rested his eyes on her white diaphanous panties. He even thought he could see the outline of her—

"See anything you like?" she teased, obviously enjoying the lust of an older man who seemed to be growing a cricket stump in his pocket.

"Oh, oh excuse me. I'm so sorry." *Damn! Why won't it go down? Go down!*

"Sorry about what? Have you been a naughty boy or something?"

"No. No. I... I just—actually, I came in to see if you had a book."

"We've got a whole shop full of them. Or were you too busy to notice?" The girl was off the ladder but still playful.

Fakih was nonplussed by the skittish, gorgeous young woman, but he got himself under enough control for the cricket stump to change back to a clothes peg, and remembered why he was there.

"I'm looking for a book by Graham Greene. *Brighton Rock*." He wasn't sure if Forbes-Smythe wanted the book or the document that had been hidden in Mariam Hussein's real Brighton, but he wasn't taking any chances of angering mighty MI6.

"Oh, Pinkie and Rose. What a tragic couple. I loved that book, I did. I used it for my master's thesis."

"You've got a Ph.D.?" He didn't know if she was a good liar or a good scholar.

"Yep. University of Reading. That's why I got a job in a bookshop. I could have gone into publishing, but they're all so poncy in that world."

Fakih didn't understand the British slang but let it slide as he found himself uncomfortably more curious about the

[13] Translation: "Phaw! I wouldn't half mind giving that one a bit of the old how's-your-father!"

girl. "I'm a journalist myself, so we've got something in common," he blurted.

"Fancy that! I'd love to be a journalist someday. But I s'pose you have to have a different degree than a Ph.D. in English Lit."

"Mine's a simple BA from Cairo University. Biology, of all things."

"Oh, so you're an Arab, then?"

"Yes. Why?"

"I've always wanted to go to that part of the world. Ever since I read Lawrence Durrell. You know, *Bitter Lemons*, *The Alexandria Quartet*."

"Yes, I have read them, too, but in Arabic. I must read the English versions one day."

"Does your wife like to read?" she asked, unblinking, staring into his eyes.

They both knew what she was doing.

"I'm not married," he replied truthfully, studiously omitting any mention of his girlfriend, a reporter for the *Guardian,* whom he'd met at a news conference over a year ago.

"You're not a homosexual, are you? I hear a lot of Arab men go both ways."

"No, not a homosexual." He laughed although wasn't sure if he should. "I'm just not married even though I'm thirty-eight. I travel too much to settle down," he half-truthed.

"You don't look thirty-eight. More like thirty, I'd say. Guess how old I am."

"Oh, I'm not very good at this. And if I get it wrong, you might be insulted."

"No, I won't. Promise."

"Okay. I'd say, um, ah, twenty-six!"

"How did you know? That's exactly right. Well, almost. I'll be twenty-six tomorrow."

"Tomorrow?"

"Yeah. One old maid coming up."

"Never. So are you having a big party?"

"Dunno. I might go out with some of the girls to the pub for a bit of a laugh."

"Ah, Miss... I don't even know your name."

"Amanda Sullivan."

"I'm Mustaffa Fakih."

He noticed her perform the quickest of double-takes when she heard the name, but it appeared she'd decided it was real. He could also see how she'd tried not to giggle.

"Well, pleased to meet you, Mustaffa."

They shook hands with staged formality.

"Amanda, this may seem, what you call a pick-up, but it is not meant to be. Could I take you out for a drink or maybe even dinner, for your birthday tomorrow?" *Fakihy, old son, the dreaded trouser asp is winning again,* he thought, to his great annoyance.

"We've only just met. So the answer, I'm sorry, is... Yes! I'd love to."

"Can I pick you up here at, say, seven?"

"That would be great."

"Okay. It's been lovely meeting you, Amanda. I'll see you tomorrow at seven." He turned to go.

"Great. Wait! Haven't you forgotten something?"

"Oh, sorry. Thank you very much."

"No, you silly git. The book! *Brighton Rock*."

"My god, I feel so stupid. Yes, do you have it?"

"Right here."

While she wrapped the book, Fakih glanced at his watch. Twelve-fifteen!

Taxi! Taxi!

CHAPTER SEVENTEEN

The Churchill is a hotel for foreign business people on expenses and, sometimes, for dishevelled, drunken camera crews escaping the delights of the Lebanese civil war. The hotel's granite-tabled reception desk is attended by men and women who, in other lives, would have been private butlers or schoolmistresses: confident, efficient, polite but, as with the British, somewhat impersonal.

"Good afternoon, sir, may I help you?" the uniformed concierge asked.

"Yes, please. I'm here for a lunch booked under the name of Delius."

"Oh, yes. You must be Mr. Fakih. They are expecting you."

The concierge did not lead Fakih to the dining room but to an elevator. "After you, sir." He bowed slightly, allowing Fakih to enter first. "They're in one of our special luncheon rooms on the third floor. Are you enjoying London, sir?"

"Oh, I live here."

"How very lucky for you. Apart from the weather, wouldn't you say, sir? Here we are. Third floor. Follow me, please, sir."

How much do I tip this fawning servant? Fakih wondered. *He could have just told me the room number. A pound? Sounds a bit cheap. Better make it two.*

"Here we are, sir. Room three oh three." The concierge tapped gently on the door with the knuckle of his third finger of his right hand and stepped back, just as he'd been taught in butlers' school.

Fakih slipped him the money as though it were a secret handshake.

The concierge bowed, thanked him politely enough, and stepped away.

"Come in, Mr. Fakih! My name is Malcolm."

Malcolm ushered him into a drab boardroom that had been laid out for lunch and, no doubt, swept for bugs. At the table sat three men.

"Thank you so much for coming at such short notice, Mr. Fakih. Let me introduce ourselves." Forbes-Smythe pointed to the man at the table closest to him. "Tommy you spoke to on the phone this morning. This is Bob, and this is Ayub. Can I get you a drink before we have lunch?"

"Just a lime and soda if you have it."

"Of course."

After Fakih sat in the sole empty chair, he studied the men around the table and wondered who the hell they were and what they wanted with him.

"I was with Mrs. Mariam Hussein last night," he said. "Tommy, is that right? Your name is Tommy? You phoned me this morning to tell me she was dead. And you knew about the Brighton rock."

"Oh, yes," Forbes-Smythe interrupted. "And the bookshop. She is what we would call a dolly-bird."

"Who?"

"Amanda Sullivan. Lovely, don't you think?"

"Is she one of you, as well?"

"Her? Let's just say we happened to see how much you enjoyed her company this morning. Please, go as our guest tomorrow night. We can get you into whatever restaurant you choose."

"So you are the British Secret Service, I assume?"

"Something like that, old boy," Forbes-Smythe said. "Now, we know you are onto the story. But you really have no idea what is going on. If you play along with us, we will give you the biggest story of your life."

"But Tommy said I might be in danger."

"That depends on you, to a certain extent. You see, we need a favour from you. You are an Arab. Smart and suspicious. Perfect, wouldn't you say, Bob?"

"Perfect, Malcolm."

Fakih glanced at the men around the table and focussed back on Forbes-Smythe. "Forgive me for saying so, but are you not also killers? I mean, the Husseins. What happened to them?"

"Very sad. But there's a lot more at stake than two Algerians. I say, why don't we eat. I'm famished."

Lunch was typical for an over-priced central London hotel: assorted cold meats, soup, warm roasted potatoes, French bread, fruit, tea and coffee. Booze was extra, but that didn't stop Ayub and Bob from ordering two decent bottles of chilled white wine at fifty pounds a bottle.

Malcolm winced but said nothing. He sipped on a rather splendid dry sherry.

"Mr. Fakih," Malcolm asked, "you know, of course, Colonel Muammar Gaddafi of Libya?"

"Of course."

"Have you ever heard of a young man from Saudi Arabia named Osama bin Laden?"

"Bin Laden. Bin Laden. Hmm. Aren't they big in construction in Saudi Arabia?"

"Quite correct, Mr. Fakih," Malcolm said. "In fact, bin Laden senior has made millions. Millions. His favourite son, Osama, is a young idealist. Well, religious fanatic, really. Now, Ayub here is a chief petty officer in the Libyan Navy."

Fakih's thoughts flashed to the *Claudia* and the story of the Libyan pistol found near a London execution scene. What in the hell were these guys up to?

Forbes-Smythe continued: "Ayub, why don't you tell Mr. Fakih what you heard yesterday about the young Osama?"

"All of it, Malcolm?"

"I'll shut you up when I have to."

"Okay. Mr. Fakih, Osama bin Laden is in Libya at this moment. For such a young man—he's only twenty-two—he has been very active in trying to recruit mercenaries to help drive out the Russians from Afghanistan."

"Why? What does he care?"

"He is what one would call a religious fanatic," Ayub said, "and he believes the Communists will march across Europe and crush all others, including Muslims, if they are not expelled from Afghanistan."

"So what's he doing in Libya?"

"We think he's trying to get more money, weapons, and fighters from Gaddafi. But he also wants something else."

"What?"

"That's enough, thanks, Ayub," Forbes-Smythe said. "Mr. Fakih, how difficult would it be for you to go to Tripoli and get an interview with Gaddafi and Mr. bin Laden?"

"That depends on the Colonel. He is very unpredictable. I do not know about bin Laden."

"Would your newspaper authorize such an assignment? You're going to report back to them at five, correct?"

Fakih was more than irritated. "Do you spy on everyone like this?"

"Only those we consider valuable or need our protection," Forbes-Smythe replied.

"And which category do I fall into?"

"Both. But let me tell you a little bit more. You see, we hear that young bin Laden is an impetuous chap. If he doesn't get what he wants, he's liable to do something quite silly. If Gaddafi doesn't give him a hundred thousand dollars, there could be an accident."

Fakih's eyes widened. "He'd assassinate Gaddafi?"

"It seems Osama is becoming an expert in making bombs and starting revolutions. You'll never guess who trained him."

"Who? The Afghans? The Syrians?"

"No. The CIA. Right, Bob?"

"Correct, Malcolm. I know the agent who handled him for a couple of years."

Forbes-Smythe continued: "I can't tell you why, but we would rather that the nasty Colonel wasn't scattered across the Maghreb by one of Osama's toys. So we want to persuade Mr. bin Laden to desist. We give him the money under the condition he leaves Libya immediately and goes straight to Afghanistan."

"And where do I fit in all of this?" Fakih asked.

"You have the declaration from Gaddafi about nuclear weapons and the name of a facilitator. Give them to me, and we'll replace them for you with perfect fakes. They should ensure your contact with Gaddafi. Ayub will help you arrange the meeting. But Ayub must stay here for the meantime. It's still a bit warm for him there. You will hint to the Colonel of Osama's intentions and ask him to have his bullies standing by. Then you will interview Mr. bin Laden, give him the money, and if he doesn't leave, Gaddafi's boys will throw him and his nasty new friends out. We don't want bin Laden killed. Or, at least, the Americans don't want him killed. They see him as a future leader in their war against the Russians. I think they've even thought up a name for his group. What is it, Bob?"

"We've thought of two names," Bob said. "The first one is the Taliban. It means 'students.' The second one is even simpler. It's called al-Qaeda. That means 'the base.' So the idea is the CIA gives them lots of money and training, and led by this bin Laden guy, they eventually drive the Russians out of Afghanistan with our guerrilla tactics."

"Mr. Malcolm, will Gaddafi go for it?" Fakih asked.

"Yes, he will. He's also, as you know, a fanatical Muslim so the idea won't be too hard to sell. And it should stop him from killing young Osama. So, Mr. Fakih, for doing us this favour you get two of the world's most exclusive interviews. But we cannot allow you to print anything yet about the nuclear angle. Not even if you've seen the proof that Gaddafi wants a bomb. We're not ready for the world to know that yet. Cheese?"

"No, thank you. Mr. Malcolm, may I ask you a question? There is a lot I don't understand about this story."

"You can ask, Mustaffa, but I can't promise to reply."

"I can't quite make the connection between the IRA and the murders or that terrible event in Belfast the other day. Are they somehow connected to this A.K. Khan?"

"I can tell you this much: there is a connection. Perhaps, one day, we will introduce you to Mr. Khan. Then you'll have an even bigger story."

"Is he the one who's going to build Gaddafi's bomb? The one the Algerians were going to steal?"

Forbes-Smythe raised his hands. "The less you know, the better at the moment. Then no one can torture the truth out of you. So what do you say, Mr. Fakih? Will you help us?"

"I don't know. It goes against all my journalistic principles, helping a spy agency. The stories are very tempting, but it's the principle of the thing. I'd also have to ask my editors in Cairo."

"Oh, they've agreed. President Sadat's office spoke to your editor personally a few minutes ago. But they'll tell you that at five o'clock, anyhow."

"And if I refuse?"

Forbes-Smythe motioned to Bob Cartwright. "Bob, what would you suggest?"

"Well, Malcolm, we could have him recalled to Cairo and serve on the night desk for the rest of his career. Or we could send him to that special hospital of yours and turn him into an alcoholic. I quite like that one. An alcoholic Muslim. Ha, ha. Or his girlfriend at the *Guardian* could be fired. Or we could simply kill him. On the other hand, he seems like a nice guy."

Mustaffa Fakih did something very rare for him. He reached across the table, poured himself a glass of wine, and drained it.

"Malcolm," Bob said, "why don't we add an incentive for Mr. Fakih?"

"Very good idea, Bob. After all, he'd be working for Her Majesty's Government. Would twenty thousand pounds be fair compensation, Bob?"

"It's the going rate, ha, ha."

"Too true, Bob. Mr. Fakih, if you agree, we will deposit twenty thousand pounds in any account of your choosing. Oh, and as I've said, dinner tomorrow will be on us." Forbes-Smythe winked. "Car, driver, the lot."

Fakih stared at the patterns on the wallpaper. No, he wasn't drunk, but his head was swimming. This was unreal! He couldn't make this stuff up if he tried. It was fiction. Couldn't be happening! They wanted to give him twenty thousand pounds. He'd have to go to Libya. Tell Gaddafi not to kill a kid called Osama who wanted to assassinate him. Give the kid a hundred thousand dollars and interview them both. If he didn't, he was dead.

How in the hell did I get myself into this mess? More importantly, how do I get out? Can I get out? Too late, Fakihy, old son. You've done it again.

"So how do I transport one hundred thousand dollars in cash without getting caught—or robbed?"

"Easy, Mustaffa." A triumphant Forbes-Smythe smiled. "Just ask Ayub. But I must inform you that you are now bound by our Official Secrets Act and this luncheon today will be classified as top secret. If anyone asks, say, like a journalist, we'll simply slap on a D-notice."

"That's where you can ban the publication of information because of threats to the security of the country," Fakih said.

"Quite correct, Mr. Fakih. And my gut tells me that if it ever came out that we gave Osama bin Laden a hundred thousand pounds, we'd be very grateful for the D-notice system."

"And when should all of this happen?"

"We thought that you should enjoy your evening with that delightful Amanda you picked up at the bookstore, then fly to Tripoli the next morning. We'll have a car pick you up. The driver will have everything else you'll need."

"No guns. I won't carry guns."

"Guns, dear boy? No. No. We don't want you to carry guns. But we want you to have a very good bang for our buck tomorrow night."

***

"That was a lovely dinner. Thank you, Mustaffa. And I love the Pinkie and Rose roses. What a thoughtful man you are."

Fakih didn't have the courage to tell her the roses had arrived in the limousine, along with a first edition of *The Alexandria Quartet* bound in a silk ribbon and an elegant card in Fakih's handwriting.

They left the restaurant and waited for a limousine.

"Where shall I ask the driver to take us?" Amanda asked. "Would you like to go to a pub? Or somewhere else perhaps, like your place?"

"Oh, of course. We can have coffee, and I think I might have some brandy hidden away somewhere."

Their hands touched lightly as the limousine headed for Chelsea. Amanda was wearing a silken, off-the-shoulder Dior gown that must have cost hundreds of pounds. Fakih didn't think Malcolm's largesse would go that far, so she must have paid for it herself. It had a subtly low neckline that highlighted the top of her glowing, eager breasts, which Fakih could not help but notice were not encumbered by a bra. Her nipples pushed hard against the silk when Fakih took her hand. He pretended not to notice.

She leaned over, brushed lightly against his Armani suit, and kissed him gently on the mouth. Fakih's clothes peg did an instant impression of the Eiffel Tower, which an aroused and wide-eyed Amanda also pretended not to notice.

When they arrived at his place, Fakih told the driver not to wait.

They entered his softly-lit flat.

"Can I get you something to drink, Amanda?"

"I'll have that brandy you mentioned if that's all right. I'll just make myself comfortable on the sofa."

Minutes later, Fakih, carrying two glasses, returned from the kitchen. "You'll get me in trouble with Allah for this." He laughed softly.

"Oh, I hope for a little more than that." As she spoke, she let the top of her gown fall away. She leaned over, slid her hands under his belt, undid the zip, and lifted Mustaffa's bulging Eiffel Tower into her mouth.

"Oh my god," he moaned, "let's go to the bedroom."

But Mustaffa had another surprise for Amanda that night. And for him, too.

When he opened the door to the bedroom, something on top of the bed moved.

Then screamed. "What the hell's going on here? Who are you? Mustaffa, what the fuck are you doing?"

"I... I... Oh, Amanda, this is Judy."

"Yes, Amanda, I'm Judy, his girlfriend. Who are you? His annual blow-job?"

"Oh, I'm sorry. It's my birthday and Mustaffa—"

"And Mustaffa couldn't keep his hands out of your knickers. Jesus, Mustaffa, you really are a wanker. Just because I said I wouldn't be here tonight you thought you could have a quickie with some tart you picked up at the pub? For god's sake, do yourself up. And, you, put your knockers away. Fuck! Fuck! Fuck! That's it, Mustaffa. I've had enough. I'm leaving. Now!"

"Well, this is embarrassing," Amanda muttered, gathering herself and also preparing to leave.

The door slammed as Judy stormed out.

"I suppose I should say thank you, but it's a hell of a way to end a birthday, Mustaffa. You really should have told me about her."

"But then you wouldn't have gone out with me. Listen, I'm sorry. Shall I get you a taxi?"

"Yes, please. At about seven in the morning."

"What do you mean?"

"You have to go to the airport quite early, and I came here to have it off with you. So let's get on with it, shall we?"

CHAPTER EIGHTEEN

September 1978

The spread of nuclear weapons was at the heart of President Jimmy Carter's peace policies. It was also at the heart of oath when he took office in 1977. It was a good guess he didn't know about the enormity of the plans of Ayub and Malcolm, but he tried hard to stop proliferation by both his country and the Soviet Union.

Israel's nuclear programme was a badly kept secret, so Jimmy Carter had to venture where fools and felons had gone before and after: the Middle East. Carter dabbled and scrabbled until his prime progenitors of potential, permanent purgatory came to a table to sign yet another dubious document, The Camp David Peace Accords.

In September 1978, Carter, Menachem Begin of Israel, and Anwar Sadat of Egypt signed the deal that pledged peace between the Jewish and Muslim states, at least until one of them changed his mind. Like the hollowed-out hagiography that was bestowed on Kissinger, the Nobel Peace Prize was accorded to Begin and Sadat just months after the signing.

Nineteen seventy-eight was a very good year for President C, but it didn't turn out so well for Sadat. On October sixth, he was assassinated. His kind of democracy was dead. In marched and slithered the tribes, the tyrants, the torturers. What could they possibly want with a ten-kiloton bomb?

Begin died of a heart attack twenty years later. The former Irgun terrorist had lived long enough to see Israel peacefully bomb, maraud, and crush any Arab resistance, not quite adhering to those long-ago Accords.

***

Jimmer Carter was still on a high in 1978 after the spectacular success of Camp David.

"I love you inside and out. Inside and out. Oh, I love them peanuts, too. Peanuuuuuts. Peanuuuuuts. Peanuts! They're nice and hot. Peanuts! I sell a lot!"

Cyrus Vance looked askance at his singing president, James Earl Carter. "Jimmy, don't you think we should talk about this Kabul thing?"

"Ah, sure, Cyrus. Say, did you know Dizzy Gillespie wrote a song called 'Salt Peanuts'?"

"No, but if you hum me a few bars..."

"Oh, that could be difficult. It's one of the most profound and complex songs ever written. Much more intricate than, say, Stravinsky. It goes something like this. 'Ooooooooh, bop-sha-bam, salt peanuts, salt peanuts! Salt peaaaaa-nuts! Pow.'"

"Very good, Mr. President, sir."

"Why, thank you ever so much, Cyrus. I used to serenade Rosalind with that one every night on the peanut farm in Georgia."

"Mr. President, Mr. President, I really think we ought to discuss Afghanistan."

"You're right, Cyrus." Carter suddenly paused and stared at the other man. "That's a silly name: 'Cyrus.'"

"It's not a silly name. It comes from Cyrus the Great, a famous Persian ruler."

"Persian? You're not related to that new fella Ruhollah Khomeini, are you?"

"No. No. It's just where the name came from."

"So what's up in old Kabul, Cyrus the Great?"

"Ah, don't do that, Mr. President. It really pisses me off."

"Cyrus! I will not have that fucking language in the Oval Office, is that clear?"

"Sorry, Jim."

"What did you call me?"

"Mr. President."

"Well, just watch it, Cy-baby, or you'll be going to Kabul. Capisce?"

"Ca-what?"

"Capisce! Didn't they teach you anything at that boarding school in Switzerland? It's Sioux for 'I'll cut your nuts off.'"

"No, I disagree. I think it's Italian for 'how would you like a knife in the front?' Anyhow, Kabul. Our ambassador there has been kidnapped."

"Who by?"

"By whom, I think you mean. Anyhow Adolf—"

"Adolph! We've got a German as our ambassador? Couldn't we get an American?"

"He is American, Mr. President. His name is Adolph Dubs. His buddies call him 'Spike.' No, don't start, Mr. President. I know Spike Jones recorded a version of the 'Peanut Vendor.' Anyhow, it appears radicals calling themselves Islamists kidnapped him. We've told our people to negotiate and not try to fight it out, but the KGB is running the operation. The hostage-takers want two of their fellow Islamists freed from prison."

"Islamists? That's a new one."

"Not to them. That's why we want our own surrogates on the ground as soon as possible."

The phone on Carter's desk lit up, and Carter picked it up.

It was the embassy in Kabul.

"He what? Who did? But I thought... Damn! My condolences to you all in Kabul." Carter replaced the phone, hung his head for a moment in prayer, and when he raised it, Vance saw traces of tears in the President's eyes.

"Mr. Dubs is dead. The Russians refused to negotiate. They tried to rescue him by fighting a gun battle. Mr. Dubs died instantly. Damn those Russians! Damn! Damn! Damn! If our surrogates can't do it, then we'll have to go in and do ourselves."

***

Soon afterwards, a still-raging Carter decided to end another crisis. On November fourth that year, Islamist militants had kidnapped fifty-two American diplomats and citizens and held them hostage for 444 days. In Iran, it was seen as the ultimate spit in the face of the much-hated Americans, especially those in the White House. In Washington, it was seen as the greatest test of Carter's term in office.

So, six months into the crisis, Carter ordered a rescue attempt. It was another colossal U.S. military embarrassment with desert-floundering helicopters breaking down and eight marines dead. Not one hostage was rescued.

But during the debacle, the Americans were setting their stage to get Osama bin Laden on their side. And they decided, finally, to call the militant opposition the Taliban, or Students.

"That's what they prefer: 'Students of Islam,'" Cyrus Vance said. "Some folks over at Defence prefer the plainer al-Qaeda, which as you know, means 'The Base.'"

"I don't care what they're called as long as they can get rid of the Russians. But aren't they very religious, too?"

"So are you, Mr. President. There's a kind of warmth that radiates from your Baptist beliefs. But I don't get a very warm feeling from these so-called Islamists."

"We can blame the damned Shah for that. My, what an evil person. No wonder the Iranians wanted anyone but him. He was callous and brutal and—"

"Yes, but he was ours," Vance said. "This new guy Ruhollah Khomeini is definitely not ours. And what's all this stuff about taking hostages? Where did they get that idea?"

"This is my last year in office, but I think it's going to be a hell of a year, Cyrus. A hell of a year. There's Khomeini, a fanatical mullah. That's what really distresses me about the KGB killing Dubs. Now everyone can take Americans hostage. And that's the good recipe. What else can go wrong?"

"Look on the bright side, Mr. C. You've always got your nuts."

A huge smile crossed Jimmy's face. "Thank you, Cyrus, old buddy."

Jimmy sang again: "If you're looking for a moral to this song, fifty million monkeys can't be wrong. Peanuts do bop do bop. Peanuts do bop do bop. Peanuts do bop do bop."

CHAPTER NINETEEN

October 1978

Osama bin Laden may have been in his early twenties, but Fakih saw a much older person. True, he already had three wives, the first when he was seventeen. That would age anyone, Fakih thought ruefully as he pondered the profanity and the pounding of a few nights previously in London. And for an ascetic, a devout and harsh interpreter of the holy Qur'an, bin Laden didn't treat himself too badly here in Tripoli.

Bin Laden's suite at the Hotel Al-Kabir overlooked the swimming pool. A gentle breeze buffeted the white curtains as the young revolutionary arose from his cushion to meet his guest. As a strict Muslim, he did not offer to shake hands but stiffly offered Fakih tea, which Fakih accepted with a little more grace.

What Fakih did not like were the three other young men with whom bin Laden shared the suite. They did not smile and turned away when introduced, but most disturbingly, they constantly fingered the triggers of the AK-47s in their laps. Fakih also noticed books, manuals, and documents on bomb-making and guerrilla tactics strewn around the main room.

"Thank you for seeing me and agreeing to an interview," Fakih said, smiling at bin Laden.

"I only agreed to meet you. Nothing else. Why should I talk to you? You, a Western lackey. You are not Islamic. You do not follow the teaching of our beloved prophet, Muhammad, Allah be praised, and may peace be upon Him. You are an infidel. Your president, Sadat, talks with the Jews. He is meeting with that friend of the devil Begin and the peanut man Carter. There will be no peace in the Middle East without Allah. These men are all apostates. I despise them, and we will spill their blood one day as ordered by Allah, may peace be upon Him."

Fakih was taken aback by this robotic diatribe. If these were the young men fighting for the Americans, whose side were they on? He tried another opening.

"Mr. bin Laden, may I ask you of your opinion of the Shia? You and I are Sunni, and the Shia broke away because they did not like the successor Allah chose for Muhammad. Will you fight the Shia as well as the other infidels?"

"This is a big mistake. While the Shia did, indeed, throw mud at the prophet, they are still Muslim. I will not declare war on any Muslim. They are our allies in our war against the capitalists and infidels."

War? Fakih hadn't heard bin Laden use that word before. This was turning into one hell of an interview, whether the young fundamentalist knew it or not. "So you intend to wage a war against the Russians?"

"Not just a war. But a holy war in the name of Allah, may peace be upon Him. We are developing tactics that will shock them. We are not afraid of death. We will defeat them and all the other infidels who do not accept that Islam is the only one true religion."

"But what about Christians and all the other religions that believe in God?"

"There is only one god, and he is Allah, may peace be upon Him. All others are false gods, and their followers must be annihilated."

Tedious doctors and journalists pontificate that the eyes are the windows to the soul. Bin-Laden's windows were closed, shut tight. Still, Fakih pushed and prodded.

"But you are going to fight for the Americans. How can you justify that, after what you have said?"

"The Americans are fools. They think we are helping them. We are taking from them. Their money, their weapons, and their training. Then we will fight them, too, when the time comes."

"When will that be?"

"When Allah, may peace be upon Him, tells us."

"How do you fight the Americans?"

"In ways they cannot imagine. That is all I will say."

"I spoke to Colonel Gaddafi yesterday, and he told me you and your friends were anxious to go to Afghanistan as soon as possible, but there appeared to be a holdup that he found difficult to understand."

"Mr. Fakih, if you fight a revolution, you must have the tools. We have the plans. I have an army of Islamic warriors two thousand strong. I have weapons and ammunition already stored secretly in Pakistan and Afghanistan. I have asked Gaddafi for several other things, but he seems to be refusing to fight for Islam. That makes him an infidel. And all infidels must die."

So Malcolm was right. This young militant was as crazy as they come. He *was* thinking of killing Gaddafi.

"Mr. bin Laden, this is only a guess, but I'm told the Colonel is trying to get nuclear weapons and when he gets them, my guess is you want him to give you some for your fight for Islam. Am I correct?"

"That is correct, but he is a long way from acquiring them. So he is of not much use to me at the moment. I am sure in the future I will be able to buy what I need."

"Of course, you come from a very wealthy family."

Fakih strolled over to a real live open window while performing his much-admired gift of being able to keep his ears to the ground while his eyes darted over the deserted streets of Tripoli below.

"My family gives me nothing. And I will take nothing from them. It is their money. Allah, may peace be upon Him, will provide me with money when He sees fit."

"So how much money do you need right now to start your operation in Afghanistan?"

"We estimate one hundred thousand American dollars."

"Surely the Americans can give that to you?"

"They have given me much money, but I have spent it all on weapons and training. They accuse me of wasting it. They say I'm just a greedy Arab who wants more. And they'll only give me more when I start their fight in Afghanistan."

"But if you do anything to Gaddafi, you'll not only never get to Afghanistan, you'll never get any more money. They won't let you out of this country for many years."

For the first time that afternoon, the arrogant, supremely confident bin Laden looked worried, even defeated. "What you say is true, Mr. Fakih. You are a very smart man for an infidel journalist."

Fakih seized the moment. "I can do better than that, Mr. bin Laden. I can save you from Gaddafi, and I can get you to Afghanistan with the money today. All you have to do is give me your word that you will not attempt to touch the Colonel and that you will leave Libya for Afghanistan tomorrow."

"How can you possibly do that?"

"Let's just say it is the will of Allah, may peace be upon Him." With that, Fakih took off his jacket, unthreaded his belt, and flipped it over to reveal a zip that ran the full length of the piece of leather. Dramatically and slowly, he pulled open the zip to reveal the money: 100 thousand-dollar bills. "The will of Allah, Osama, the will of Allah."

Bin Laden took the money and counted it carefully.

"Do we have a deal, Osama? Don't touch Gaddafi and leave for Afghanistan tomorrow?"

"Yes, yes. We have a deal."

"I'll need you to write a note to that effect. Just as a precaution."

Bin Laden took his eyes off the money to look at Fakih. “But what’s to stop me killing you and leaving without writing anything down?”

“Oh, didn’t I tell you? Colonel Gaddafi knows of every move I am making. And you see this piece of wire? It’s a radio antenna. Look out the window. Yes. Those are tanks. If you double-cross me, you will die. You have a lot to learn yet, Mr. bin Laden, but I think you’ll make a good start by writing the note.”

Again, bin Laden fell silent. He took a sip of tea, opened a drawer, pulled out a piece of hotel stationery, and with his left hand, began to write.

***

Two days later, the Taliban fired their first rocket at a Russian tank. It was a perfect hit.

CHAPTER TWENTY

1981

Ronnie the Reagan soaked his head in sump oil before every television appearance. When the nation saw their Commander in Chief, they knew he cared enough to be as immaculately groomed as he knew how. He didn't use make-up on his face but smeared peanut butter over his brow and cheekbones. It was an old actor's trick he'd learned from his second-rate glory days in Hollywood. It gave the face a natural-looking tan, especially in black and white. The only problem occurred in the summertime when swarms of flies would necessitate up to a hundred takes for one close-up. But, my, Ron looked handsome when they finally got what the director of photography called "a keeper." Ron wasn't sure what that meant, and the director didn't say it very often in his presence, but the stand-in told Ron he heard it all the time.

"Are you ready, Mr. President?" the aspiring-pole-vaulting opportunistic wing-stander Secretary of State Alexander Haig asked. "If you don't feel like making the speech, I could do it for you," he offered, sounding innocent enough.

"No, it's okay, Al. I'm ready. Say, Al, have I ever told you about the pianist Al Haig? Used to play bebop until he tried kill his wife. Say, that's not you, is it, Al? Did you use to play bebop with Charlie Parker before you became secretary of state?"

"Do I look black to you, Mr. President?"

"There you go again. Is Stan Getz black? Is Woody Herman? Is Benny Goodman? They're all white. And so is the pianist Al Haig, so you could be him. Have you tried to kill your wife? See. Now sit down at the piano and hit me with a nice boogie-woogie."

"But I can't play the piano!"

"Don't start that fibbing with me, Al. I don't like it. Your name's Al Haig, so blow me away with a few choruses of "It Must Be Jelly Cuz Jam Don't Shake Like Dat."

"Holy Jesus."

"Okay, a hymn would be nice."

"No, I meant: what is that terrible smell? It seems to be coming from... from—"

"From where, Al?"

"Ohh. Never mind, Mr. President," after which Al Haig fisted out a very loud and very bad version of "Chopsticks."

"See. See. I knew you were Al Haig. You can't fool the old gipper. I know, why don't we get Stan Kenton in here one day to do his famous 'Peanut Vendor.' Sort of a tribute to my predecessor. You can replace Stan on piano, and I'll do the singing."

"Oh Jesus," Haig said.

"That's a great idea, Mr. Secretary. Let's say a prayer to the Almighty before I go on television. By the way, when do I go on television?"

"In ten seconds."

> "Holy moly, roly poly, amen. Good evening, my fellow Americans. Tonight I want to talk to you about something very important that has come to our attention here at the White House. My secretary of

> state, Al Haig, who is also a well-known jazz pianist and lady-killer... Uncle Al, the Kiddies' Pal, we call him around here... Anyhow, I digress. I guess I'm still an old cowhand at heart. Aw, shucks, but you know that. But this is serious."

Here, the script called for the cameraman to zoom into a close-up of Ron, but the operator noticed what he thought were drops of skin falling off Ron's face. Was the President going to announce he has leprosy? No, it was only the peanut butter melting under the hot TV lights. But the cameraman stayed on a wide shot all the same.

> "We have heard Pakistan is preparing to build a nuclear weapon. Now, we know that India and Pakistan proposed a non-proliferation treaty. That's nice. The Indians went ahead and built their bomb they called 'Smiling Buddha.' Mighty cute, doncha think? The Pakis—I mean the Pakistanis—have been in touch with the Chinks... Ah, ah—people of the Chinese persuasion—and General Muhammad Gadarmy of Lebanon. Wait a minute. Al, have you been screwing with my autocue again?"

Darty-eyed Al Haig looked askance. Even distrustful.

> "Sorry, folks. I think that should read Colonel Muhammad Gaddafi of Liberia. Well, I want to warn them all that the United States will not sit by and watch them enrich uranium to anything above five percent. There will be grave consequences if they do. What do I mean by that? We will apply various methods of draconian dissuasion. First, I will send my Secretary of State Al Haig to each country and insist all its leaders listen to him as he plays his very own rendition of that lovely old song my mommy used to sing: 'If I Give Up the Saxophone, Will You Come Back to Me?'

> "Should that fail to stop these rogue states, I will have no option to bomb them back into the Stone Age, not that they aren't all there now. So, China, Pakistan, and Libya, you have been warned. It's either Al's way or the runway, with fucking great swarms of B-52s taking off to drop thousands of pounds of bombs on you. Naaa. Just kidding! We'll nuke you instead. Thank you. And God Bless..."

Haig had his eyes on Ron's job from the moment of the inauguration on January 20, 1981, but he was intrigued by this pianist notion of Reagan's and thought he might be better at the saxophone. So he began taking lessons from a jazz legend Al thought was still alive—tenor saxophonist John Coltrane. Everyone in the White House told him Coltrane was the greatest ever. What they didn't mention was that he had died twenty-five years prior.

Haig had looked him up in the phone book, and this John Coltrane said he'd never played an instrument in his life. Haig thought the great man was taking the piss, so he descended on his Harlem shack with a squad of cops, held a gun to Mr. John Coltrane's head, and yelled: "Teach me, you son-of-a bitch, or I blow your fucking teeth out and you'll never play 'Swanee' again."

"'Swanee'? That ain't no Coltrane tune, man. How 'bout I teach you how to play 'Giant Steps'?"

"'Giant Steps'?"

"It's got these chords that shift through tritones and major thirds with a preponderance of arpeggios through the changes."

Coltrane was, of course, spewing jazz gibberish for the buffoon standing in front of him. But Al knew when he was being taken for an idiot, which was twenty-four-seven, so he didn't notice an ever-so-slight sleight.

Even so, Haig decided this guy Coltrane was overrated and went in search of anyone who taught the ukulele—the ukulele with the plastic-box chord-finder at the top of the fret. He could plunk out "I've Got a Lovely Bunch of Coconuts" within half an hour. He'd be a musical sensation.

What did that fucking John Coltrane know? *Jazz genius, my ass*.

As Haig plucked merrily away in his office, an aide rushed in. "The President's been shot! The President's been shot!"

"Who did it? The Chinks? The Pakis? Get the B-52s rolling."

"Not unless you want them to bomb Colorado. No, it was some white guy called Hinkley. Mr. Reagan is in the hospital now. And Press Secretary Larry Speakes is giving a news conference about his successor who—"

The aide never finished the sentence. Haig hurled the ukulele over his head, leaped over his desk, sprinted to the pressroom, slammed Speakes out of the way as if he were a defensive lineman for the Pittsburgh Steelers, and announced that he was now in charge of the nation. This was no time to consider the constitutional order of succession: the Speaker, the Chief Justice. No. It was King Al, the ukulele player's pal, who would now run the nation.

First item of his agenda: bomb someone. Such as the Libyans or the Pakis.

I know, the Libyans. That fucking Gaddafi needs a good shit-kicking. I hear he's helping the Pakis with their bomb. And he blew up some of our good folks in a disco in Berlin. Right, then. This'll stop him.

***

"Mr. President. You're back."

"My back? What about it?"

"No, I mean: welcome back. How do you feel?"

"With my right hand just like you, you old son-of-a-gun."

"So you like my plan to knock the shit out of Gaddafi?"

"Plan? What plan?"

"The one where we send in a couple of hundred F-111s and blow his military installations to pieces."

"Seeing you did such a good job in my absence, how can I refuse you, old friend. Off you go."

Would you like to hear me sing 'Swanee' with my ukulele before I go?"

"Oh, how thoughtful. That's my favourite all-time Negro spiritual, Al. No, thanks."

***

So the bombers blew much of the Colonel's military installations to matchwood, along with a hundred civilians and three of Gaddafi's kids.

Al and Ron had done real good.

CHAPTER TWENTY-ONE

Khan was now a happy man. And very rich. Gaddafi had been so enraged by the U.S. bombings that he doubled his supply of stolen Niger yellowcake and cash to Khan to finish the facilities in both Libya and Pakistan. Khan, meanwhile, had become even more esurient, rapacious, gluttonous—even edacious. That last one was a new honour bestowed upon him by world peace champions Iran and North Korea. Khan would slip them a bomb or two when nobody was looking. But when Gaddafi finally got his bomb, the Colonel had a different plan from the Pakistanis.

At around 7:00 p.m. on the night of December 21, 1988, Libyan operatives brought down Pan Am Flight 103 over Lockerbie, Scotland, killing 270 people. Bin Laden and his friend Mullah Omar had just about finished kicking the Russians out of Afghanistan. Khan begrudgingly admitted the Americans had masterminded that one very well. Thirty thousand dead Russians. The rest: humiliated and on the run. And the Americans had helped bin Laden and Omar establish an effective set of training camps for more mujahideen[14] along the Pakistan-Afghan border. Khan boasted he was less than two years away from detonating his first bomb. The Pakistani Air Force had begun modifying some of its fighter planes to carry nuclear weapons, and the Chinese had sold them M-11 missiles to give a choice of delivery systems.

But Gaddafi had his eyes on bin Laden. Could he get the now thirty-three-year-old guerrilla leader to carry out the most audacious plot yet? Detonate an atomic bomb over Washington.

The Pakistanis were so thrilled with A.K. Khan's work that in 1990 they gave him the "Man of the Nation" award, failing to publicly acknowledge that Khan had stolen, cheated, and cajoled a dozen countries to help him, both as a freelancer and as a dedicated Pakistani and Muslim. In return, he became immeasurably wealthy.

In London, none of this had gone under the radar. Malcolm Forbes-Smythe was no longer head of MI6. He had been promoted to Special Advisor to the Prime Minister and the Armed Forces of Great Britain and Northern Ireland. No one outranked him in the military, the civil service, or the police. He was Deputy God under the PM, which was not often since like most men, gay or straight, he bore no lust for Margaret Thatcher. But that John Major, well, he could be different.

Of the coterie who had bowled A.K.'s middle stump a decade ago, Chief Petty Officer Ayub el-Sahafat had kissed and made up with his Colonel and was working so many sides of the arms trade that even Malcolm was losing track. But Ayub never lost track of A.K. Khan. He also supervised the shipping of yellowcake through the Libyan port of Benghazi.

Ayub didn't want a promotion. His neck was enough. And as long as the construction of the two nuclear plants continued and there was no bomb, he was safe. After that? He had so much money stashed in banks around the globe

---

[14] Arabic term that broadly refers to Islamic guerillas who engage in jihad.

that he wasn't bothered. Except for that thing with bin Laden. Would they really try to blow up Washington?

Bin Laden had changed. Ayub had met him several times on his trips to Pakistan. He had never liked him, but now bin Laden had a messianic menace. He called himself the leader of al-Qaeda and left the Taliban to Mullah Omar. Ayub admitted bin Laden freaked him out.

Ayub wondered if the British and the Americans knew of bin Laden's plan. Washington was one of Ayub's main sources of income, especially when he ratted on some of the Colonel's activities, such as Lockerbie. But he hadn't yet let on about the bomb plot. Malcolm had said a long time ago they would get the bombs from Gaddafi before he could use them. But things change.

Things change.

***

Ayub told Gaddafi he needed to make a trip to London to set up another shipment, and the next day he was in Malcolm's new office in Whitehall. Days earlier, Malcolm had ceremoniously sunk his beloved Temeraire with an ironic bottle of Black Bush Irish whiskey

"Malcolm, I'm not sure how to tell you this, but I've been speaking to bin Laden."

"And what does the scrawny beanpole, Yemeni-born, Saudi-enriched, crazed-follower of Allah have to say to a midget Libyan?"

"He has this plan. Well, Gaddafi has the plan, and he's going to get bin Laden to carry it out."

"Do go on, old son."

You know that plant he and Khan are building? I mean, the two in Libya?"

"Of course. Not too far from completion. Khan is crowing like a victorious cock, if you'll pardon the expression. We may have to shut him up. I do so dislike braggarts. Especially crooked, greedy ones."

"Like that doctor what's-his-name?"

"Oh. Miles. He died in prison. Anyhow, this plot. Does it involve Gaddafi's bomb by any chance?"

"Yes, how did you know?"

"I didn't. But remember our old CIA friend Bob Cartwright?"

"I remember him choking me to death. Yes."

"Bob's retired now. But he's been in Pakistan, too, doing a bit of nosing around for me. The CIA in Islamabad is worried about the training camps bin Laden is running. Seem to be very anti-Western and drawing all kinds of scrofulous Arabs from all over the world. With the Russians gone, we were wondering what they're up to. Our Intel people say bin Laden's been talking about bombing a U.S. ship, maybe in the Mediterranean. The Pakistani government is fucking useless. It lies through its teeth to us all the time, even about their bomb and the importance of Khan. Who do they think we are? Anyhow, we think their security service, the ISI[15], is actually helping bin Laden form his terrorist cells."

"I don't understand. Why?"

"Power, my dear Ayub, power. The generals and the ISI run the country. If they run bin Laden, too, they run their very own terror group and can hold any of us to ransom at any time."

"What are you going to do about it?"

"Quite a lot, dear boy. Quite a lot. But finish telling me about your little plot."

"Gaddafi wants bin Laden to explode a nuclear bomb over Washington."

"Does he? Indeed," Malcolm said. "What a naughty Colonel. We thought they were going to do the Empire State Building or the World Trade Centre. But nuke Washington? That's a bit rich, don't you think? Any idea how?"

"My guess would be a suicide team on a scheduled commercial flight. A 747 refitted with a hidden carrying bay."

---

15 Inter-Services Intelligence, the premier intelligence agency of Pakistan.

"So now we're not only going to have to carpet-bomb your very boring desert but hunt around for one of your 747s?"

"Why don't we just kill bin Laden?"

"Too late now. Too late to kill the Colonel, too. Too many other crooks in the wings, dear boy. Unless..."

"Unless what?"

"Do you remember our lad Billy we sent to join the IRA?"

Ayub winced at the mention of the disastrous gun-running fiasco. "Of course. That fucking *Claudia* thing nearly got me killed. And that stupid A.K. with his dirty bomb. Yes, I remember Billy. Why?"

"Chief Petty Officer el-Sahafat, Billy McFadden or, as we know him, Major William McFadden of Her Majesty's First Battalion, the Parachute Regiment, is now Billy McFadden, Commander in Chief of Operations for the entire IRA."

"The boss?"

"The boss."

"So you run the IRA?"

"Yes, but we let them go about their own nasty business most of the time so no one gets suspicious."

"So Billy's still killing innocent people and soldiers," Ayub said.

"It's funny how quickly we all got used to it. Especially Billy. I suppose it's in the blood."

"What?"

"Killing, dear boy, killing."

"So where does he come into the al-Qaeda plot?"

"You see, Ayub, old son, before the politicians work out some kind of peace accord in Northern Ireland, Billy will have to be extracted before the truth comes out. Either the Irish will kill him or someone else will."

"And who's that someone else, Malcolm?"

"You."

"Me?"

"You. Now, don't look so startled. You won't have to actually kill him yourself. But I do need you to organize a meeting with Khan, bin Laden, Billy, and Gaddafi."

"Where?"

"Oh, I thought somewhere very private, like Speakers' Corner in Hyde Park."

"You're not serious?"

Malcolm was in full spy-boss mode. His speech sped up and so did his mind, racing nearer to his nefarious conclusion far away from the madding crowd at Speakers' Corner.

"Of course not, you great pillock. It would have to be in Libya—as long as we can get Billy there. And this is where you come in, Ayub. Bob and I will guide you through it, but you must get the whole group to agree on the plane to nuke Washington. Gaddafi can supply the money and his bomb. Khan will have to be on board to decide the technical stuff, like precisely when to drop it, from what height, depending on wind and airspeeds. Bin Laden will be director of operations and in charge of getting a flight crew. We'll tell Billy that the IRA have decided he's a traitor and will first torture the names of operatives out of him. Next, kill his parents before his eyes and then tar and feather Billy, tie him to a post, set him on fire, and let the night creatures do the rest. None of this is true, of course, but it should convince him to take a vacation on your idyllic women- and booze-laden beaches."

"But why would he go along with a plan to bomb Washington? Half the IRA funding comes from there."

"Quite true. But Billy is not a very good flier. Needs lots of medication. Just like Khan, only worse. But we'll tell Billy the purpose of the mission is to bomb Stormont Castle, the seat of government in Northern Ireland. Once the plane takes off, Billy will have no idea where the hell it is. Besides, the 747 will not actually reach Washington."

"What do you mean?"

"We have some excellent Arabic-speaking chaps who will be disguised as ground crew. They will load the nuclear bomb onto a Libyan Arab 747, but they'll add a tiny but powerful device of their own. It will go 'boom' while the plane is somewhere over the Atlantic, and everyone dies. The atomic bomb drops to the floor of the ocean, and we are rid of the dreadful bore A.K. Khan and the insane bin Laden."

"And Billy."

Malcolm smiled. "Yes, Billy goes, too. Neat, don't you think?"

"But you've forgotten Gaddafi."

"A few minutes after the 747 takes off, our very good friends the Americans and we will launch waves of Polaris missiles from submarines off the coast and blow both of the Colonel's facilities to dust. If you choose, you can either shoot him or let him ponder his stupidity for the rest of his life. I find the latter quite attractive, don't you?"

"And the Pakistanis?"

"They will be told that Gaddafi offered Khan ten million dollars for his direct assistance and the greedy man could not resist. Having seen what we will have done to Gaddafi's installations, they won't be too eager to complain about the loss of the father of their Islamic bomb."

Ayub had never seen Malcolm Forbes-Smythe so confident or assured. Here he was, about to foil one of the world's great terrorist attacks and wipe out the terrorists and some encumbrances at the same time. It reminded him of his first impression of bin Laden, and that made him rather uneasy.

***

The first mistake was a huge one. Malcolm Forbes-Smythe was so shocked at his incompetence that he pondered going celibate for a quarter of a second, came to his senses, and started on a new plan.

Libyan Arab Airlines didn't have any 747s or long-distance planes of any kind. And they didn't fly to the United States. *Oops*! Okay, so there was an airstrip next to the real nuclear base in Libya. The bomb could be loaded onto a regular Airbus. Maybe Khan could take it as carry-on. It weighed only five tons and was three feet long. His ego alone was twice those dimensions. No, better send it as accompanied baggage.

"Anything to declare?"

"Just this atomic bomb."

"Oh, that's all right then, sir. No duty on atomic bombs. Carrying any cigarettes or alcohol, are we, sir? Because I might have to charge you duty on them."

"No."

"Fine. You're clear to go. Welcome to Britain."

Years in the profession told Forbes-Smythe that it probably wouldn't be that simple. So the plane lands at Heathrow with an A-bomb on board. Only it's marked FRAGILE: ELECTRONIC GOODS. HANDLE WITH CARE.

Though he detested the Irish, except the Northern type, he wallowed in the poems of Yeats. That "Second Coming" was prescient and eponymous—in Malcolm's mind, at least. As Yeats had implied, it was time to summon the falcon.

Forbes-Smythe picked up the phone and dialled.

"Police, Heathrow."

"Could I speak with Chief Superintendent Williamson, please?"

"I'm sorry, he's in a meeting. Can you leave a message?"

"No. Get him out of the meeting."

"And just who might you be, sir?"

"Malcolm Forbes-Smythe, that's who."

"Oh, I'm sorry, sir. I'll get him right away."

Seconds later, the falcon landed.

"Teddy, Malcolm. Will you be in your office in, say, two hours? Oh. I'd prefer you were. Yes. I thought I'd pay you a visit. Got something on my mind. No. No. Nothing like that. I don't care what you and your boys get up to after hours. So I'll see you shortly. And, Teddy, be a good chap and put out that awful pipe before I get there."

"Tommy, feel like a drive in the country? I'd rather not use one of the staff lads for this. I think we go very carefully from here on."

"Do you want back-up, Malcolm?"

"Daylight. We're both armed. Good radio contact. No, I think we're okay."

"Sorry, Malcolm, but I disagree. If we have to go carefully on this one, be silly not to start now, don't you think?"

"You're right. Is that old painting van still around?"

"They've got a new one now, sir, with all new kinds of gear. I'll get them over here right away."

Just as Malcolm had feared, Chief Superintendent Teddy Williamson's office stank of old pipe tobacco. The constant scream of jets and the ghastly warm tea made a delightful start to the meeting.

Williams was no Bill Playter, who had died of prostate cancer a couple of years previously, and Malcolm had not yet found a replacement he could trust. So he did most of the police work himself. A job he loathed. The police were generally vastly below his intellectual level, venal and lazy. But they did have the propensity to do as they were told, rightly or wrongly. And it was wrong what Malcolm needed.

"It's coming in from Tripoli with a very special cargo that I do not want British customs to see. You are one of the few people in this business I can trust completely," Malcolm said.

Tommy had heard this line before and knew Malcolm was on the bullshit trail, but he kept a straight face.

"Teddy, something very big is happening. If you help me, we may both save thousands of lives. And, of course, the PM will hear about it when I write my report. How does 'Sir Edward' sound? Ha, ha. You never know, Teddy. You never know."

Tommy was in puke-mode now, but Teddy had fallen for it. Amazing. Him a senior copper and all.

"Malcolm, the way I see it, I can get a couple of my lads to join the unloading crew. Get me the weigh bill number of your consignment, and they'll it whisk off to a police security area even before customs knows the plane has landed. What should we do with it?"

Copper Teddy bowed imperceptibly as Malcolm re-took the floor.

"Tommy Beecham here"—Malcolm pointed to Tommy—"will come and pick it up with some of my men. What time do you suggest, Teddy?"

"There's a customs shift change at eight every night. That's probably the best time, when they're rushing off to the pub or trying to get their papers in order for the long night ahead. Even so, I can arrange a little distraction or scare for them. Perhaps a bomb hoax in customs shed two. That always gets them excited, especially these days. Or I can have one of my officers pretend to give birth in terminal three if you like. Or both." Teddy smiled.

"Whatever you think is best, Teddy." Malcolm returned the smile. "You've been a great help. I'll be in touch in a couple of days. One or two more things to sort out."

Teddy went all formal. "Mr. Forbes-Smythe, can I ask you what really is in that consignment?"

"I can't tell you right now, Teddy, but it's not drugs if that's what you were worried about."

"The thought did cross my mind, I don't mind admitting."

"No. No drugs, so rest easy, Teddy. Or should I say, Sir Edward?"

"Yes, yes. Right. Thank you, Malcolm. You can rely on me."

"You'd better be right, my friend, or they'll find you in Finsbury Park, too," Malcolm muttered under his breath. "Cheerio, then."

"Cheerio."

It was dusk by the time Malcolm and Tommy got back to Whitehall. A crimson glow had settled on the Thames, and Malcolm momentarily thought it was time he wallowed in the Turners in the Tate Gallery again. Or was it the National

Gallery? No, that gorgeous Monet hung in the entrance. Maybe that fucker Khan could buy it for him before he went on his one-way journey. Wait a minute, old son. Would Khan like his last fifty million quid in art? Why the fuck not? Perfect. *That's what we'll do then. Pay the little shit with an I.O.U. from Sotheby's, and I get the loot. Lovely, old son, lovely. Nice little Christmas surprise for Jeremy, too.*

Now then, where do I get a jumbo jet that I can rip apart and fit with an atomic bomb?

"Tommy, does the Foreign Office ever charter jumbo jets from BA for relief flights and that sort of thing? You know, humanitarian nonsense?"

"On the odd occasion. But generally something smaller than a 747. But you don't need to do that, Malcolm. The PM has the power to commandeer whatever he wants in times of emergency."

"Who decides that?"

"I'm looking at him."

"Oh, right! I forgot. What a pillock."[16]

A stupid penis is how Malcolm regarded the current prime minister, John Major. Still, the fussy, fuzzy PM had a role in Malcolm's master plan.

"Hello, Mr. Major. All right. John, then. Listen, John, I need your approval to hire—but you haven't heard who. Right. That's why you hired me. Your approval code, John? It's for that, too? Yes, of course, I should have it along with the military and Her Majesty. Not over the phone. Of course. Oh, you'll send the deputy PM over with it in a few minutes? Thank you, John. Goodbye." Forbes-Smythe replaced the receiver.

Huh! Now I can blow up the universe!

---

[16] "Pillock" is one of those fifteenth-century nouns that got lost in translations over the centuries. Originally, it meant "penis." Now it means "stupid."

"Tommy, when the lackey comes with the codes, would you order me one British Airways 747, please. To take away. Ha, ha."

"Where do we want this 747, sir?"

"It's going to have to go to an RAF base for that refit. Get one of those boffins with the huge moustaches to find a spot, would you, Tommy? They'll have to find a hangar big enough. Get BA to fly the thing. I don't believe the RAF uses Boeing 747s. Toffee-nosed gits. That poses another problem. Who flies this thing to Washington? Or, at least, part of the way there?"

"Didn't Mr. Cartwright mention that some of bin Laden's followers were learning to fly?"

"Christ. Put one of those madmen in charge of a 747? They're not going that far, are they? When's Bob due back?"

"He's back tonight, Malcolm."

"Excellent. Have him drop by tomorrow, please. Tommy, what else have we to do tonight?"

"We haven't mentioned the IRA and Billy McFadden."

***

The four men wearing black hoods with slits for eyes were menacing enough. But it was what they said that scared the shit out of Billy McFadden.

They were huddled in a barn near Crossmaglen, with just a bare table and a kerosene lamp flickering an eerie light.

"So this friend of ours was in Brixton prison. He was a computer expert in the city, so he was. But he got greedy and was caught siphoning off a few million quid. The silly bastard bought a house in Hampstead and a yacht. So they put him away for five years. This year he was up for parole. They turned him down but offered him a sweet deal. If he could convert the prison records to computer disks, they'd cut a year off. Before you could say 'the Queen's a lesbo,' boyo cracked it. But funny thing, Billy, is that one of our lads in there made him another offer. Run your name through his fancy new computer, or his fancy new house would burn to the ground. And do you know what, Billy? There was no trace of your name."

"Oh, lads. Lads, it's obvious. He left it off in the transfer. I've shown you my papers. They're genuine, lads. You know that. And what the fuck were you doing checking on me without my express permission?" Billy had regained enough composure to act angry.

"You know, Billy, we got to thinking after three of our operations were stopped by the fuckin' Brits. They'd been tipped off. And only the five of us knew about them."

Billy recognized the voice of IRA boss McGuigan.

"So, Billy, we did some investigating on our own."

Jesus, Billy thought. *They're right. I went too far. Fuck.*

"Anyhow, Billy, our computer friend said he would check with the prison's written records to make sure he hadn't left any other names off. He hadn't, Billy. Not one. The trouble was, Billy, your name was never entered anywhere in Brixton. So we did one more thing. We kidnapped one of those SAS bastards, and we started cutting his balls off with a pair of scissors. I'm surprised you didn't hear him screaming. Jesus, he was loud, so we gagged him and kept on snipping away. We got one ball right off, didn't we, Mr. X?"

Billy knew for certain that Mr. X was Seamus Findlay: The Kneecapper.

Seamus nodded. "Yelled like a banshee until we gagged him."

"Anyhow, Billy, we thought we'd cut his willy off next. That's when he cracked. Nodded his head furiously, he did. So we took the gag off, but I kept the scissors right on his dick. And do you know what he told us, Billy? He said the commander in chief of the IRA was an MI6 man who infiltrated us ten years ago by shooting dead three of his own mates in a taxi. He was a legend. And if the SAS ever caught him, they would kill him themselves."

Billy knew the jig was up. And so was he. "All right, you Fenian bastards. All I am required to do is give you my name and rank. I am Major William McFadden, First Battalion, Her Majesty's Parachute Regiment."

"So you're a fuckin' para, are you? Well, para-fucking Major Billy, we have a special treat for fuckin' paras. You bastards will never get away with killing thirteen unarmed civilians on Bloody Sunday[17] no matter what you crooked fuckin' courts of inquiry decide. You know the tradition of the IRA, Billy. We kneecap traitors. Seamus is a butcher. Seamus, get the chainsaw."

The other three grabbed Billy and bound him to a pole in the barn. They shoved a bunch of straw in his mouth.

Seamus fired up the chainsaw.

Billy screamed but all that did was make him choke on the straw.

Seamus was, indeed, an expert. The right kneecap came away within seconds. Seamus slipped and gouged a chunk out of Billy's leg before he moved to the second kneecap that, again, he tore through in a hail of blood and bone splinters in another five or six seconds. Next, amid the smell of burning flesh and the sound of his own choking, Billy recognized the stench of hot tar boiling in a bucket over several lanterns.

They lifted the bucket over his head, and as it streaked its way down his naked body, the tar blistered and melted Billy's blackened skin.

The pain was gone. Shock had supplanted it.

In true Irish tradition, the IRA men fluttered duck feathers all over the gruesome black, bent, silent former commander in chief. As a final act, McGuigan kicked over the lanterns and set the barn on fire.

"Fucking Brits will never learn, will they?"

They said goodbye to their former leader.

McGuigan waited until they got back to Belfast, and then he phoned the Crossmaglen Army barracks. He told them there was a package they should collect in a burned-out barn outside Crossmaglen.

---

[17] Massacre on January 30, 1972, when British soldiers shot unarmed civilians during a protest march in Londonderry, Northern Ireland.

"It's one of yours. We called him Billy. You called him Major William McFadden." He hung up.

"This calls for a wee drink, eh, lads?"

CHAPTER TWENTY-TWO

British Airways announces the departure of 747 flight BA two one seven for Washington Dulles Airport. Would all passengers please proceed through security to the boarding gate B fifteen."

"Heathrow ground control. BA charter heavy zero niner eight, please continue taxi to outer perimeter runway five niner left and hold for takeoff for Washington Dulles. Tower will take over."

"Roger."

"BA heavy zero niner eight Heathrow tower. You will be followed on the same flight path by BA heavy two one seven. Separation will be ten. I repeat, ten miles."

"Roger."

Malcolm Forbes-Smythe, Tommy Beecham, Bob Cartwright, and Chief Petty Officer Ayub el-Sahafat listened to the communications patched into Malcolm's new, but as yet shipless, office from Heathrow.

It had taken two months and four days to reach this moment. The RAF balked at having to fit a secret bomb bay in the belly of a BA 747, but the Prime Minister ordered the RAF and the mechanics to sign the Official Secrets Act. They fitted the plane with the most beautiful bomb bay since

Hiroshima. Malcolm dubbed Khan's device the "Enola Very Gay."[18]

The transfer from the Libyan Arab Airbus went smoothly until the bomb was moved from the secure police area at Heathrow to the RAF base at Brize Norton.

An officious customs officer whined out his order. "I don't care who you are. That cargo is not leaving this airport without customs clearance."

Chief Superintendent Teddy Williamson's knighthood was disappearing with astonishing velocity. He'd forgotten about the exit formalities and the two customs officers on the gate.

Malcolm Forbes-Smythe, Tommy Beecham, Bob Cartwright, and Chief Petty Officer Ayub el-Sahafat went around to the back of the long-haul truck sporting a JIFFY DELIVERIES logo on its side.

"Open the back door, please, sir."

Malcolm had taken extra precautions with this delivery. Along with the regular MI6 agents in the front seat, two more heavily armed men guarded the atomic bomb in the back of the van. Two plain cars—a black Rover and a tan Ford with four more agents—were parked about a hundred yards up ahead, ready to do top-and-tail for the ninety-mile drive to RAF Brize Norton.

"Damn. The lock is jammed. Hang on a minute, officer." The agent stalled as his partner softly radioed for instructions.

Tommy relayed the grim information to his boss. "Malcolm, there's trouble at the customs gate."

"That fucking berk, Williamson. Get him now, Tommy. Tell him to fix it now. Blow up the whole fucking airport for all I care, but fix it!"

"My god, I didn't think of that gate," a stunned and unknighted Williamson said.

"Bill, Marjorie, Jennie, Tom. Get in four cars. Lights and sirens. Customs gate forty-two. Arrest the customs men

[18] The original Enola Gay was the U.S. Stratofortress that dropped the A-bomb on Hiroshima.

on charges of receiving stolen goods. Handcuff them. And bring them back to me. Go!"

Meanwhile, the customs men were getting impatient and suspicious. "I think we should radio for back-up, what d'ya say, Jack?"

"Aye. Something's not right here. Unless you can get that open with your keys in two minutes, we'll have some lads break it down."

"Give us a break, guv. I'll get it in a minute."

"Two minutes."

"Hello, control. We have a suspicious van attempting to leave gate forty-two without papers. Could you send over a cutting team right away?"

"Roger."

The customs break-in team was a mile away when they got the call. In the distance, they heard the scream of police sirens. Just another night at one of the world's busiest airports.

"That didn't take you chaps long," a slightly drop-jawed customs officer said.

The agents in the back of the van flipped off their safety catches and prepared to shoot.

"Only if you have to," the agent in the front whispered. "The cavalry's on its way."

What a fucking disaster, Malcolm thought. *We'll have two dead customs men, a shitload of cops all over us, and one atomic bomb to explain. Get us out of this one, Malcolm told himself.*

"All I've got to do is cut off the handle. Dead simple. Where the hell are those cops going? Anyhow, here goes."

In one move, a hastily-summoned mechanic sheared off the handle, wrenched down on the lock, and the doors fell open. It took a second for him to adjust to the light and to realize he was staring at the barrels of two machine guns.

"Holy—"

He never finished the prayer. The screech of tires and the police loudspeakers startled him and the customs officers even more.

"Stand where you are. You, in the uniforms. You are all under arrest. Do not move or we will shoot."

The police conveniently found stolen goods in each of the customs men's lockers, and they were held overnight for a bail hearing in the morning.

The mechanic was put in a separate cell and would be held on more serious charges after police found the kilo of cocaine they had hidden in his truck.

Malcolm wondered if he was wrong about Williamson, after all.

The convoy pulled away from gate forty-two, turned west, and reached the airbase in just under two hours.

***

A.K. Khan entered Malcolm's office cautiously. His hip still gave him trouble in cold weather, and his testes swelled enormously at the most embarrassing moments. Worst of all, he now hated cricket.

"Ahem," he said.

"Oh, A. K., do come in," Malcolm said. "How're they hanging?"

"By the neck, still... I presume you mean our military's method of execution."

"Oh, yes, that, too. So you've had a look at the work the chaps are doing at Brize Norton. Any complaints?"

"No, they are doing an excellent job. I have also refined a remote control mechanism so I can detonate the bomb from my own seat if I have to. But what I do not understand, Mr. Malcolm, is why the British government is going along with the plot. I mean, there could be tens of thousands of dead Americans. It could start World War Three. Me, I do not care. I've got many, many millions from this project. But it makes no sense that the British are involved."

"Let me ask a question, A.K. Do you care what happens to bin Laden?"

"No. I do not like him. He is very arrogant."

"Do you care what happens to his followers who'll fly the plane?"

"Not in the least. I do not know them. And they are not true Islamists. I think they do it for sex."

"Sex?"

"You know, the virgins and all that poppycock."

"And Gaddafi?"

"He has paid me in full, so I have no further use of him."

"Before I let you into a little secret, can you set the bomb from the ground?" Malcolm asked.

"I can, but it wouldn't be as reliable. Besides, I don't think bin Laden would fly without me. He's a very suspicious man."

"Could you drop it without them knowing?"

"Difficult. The aircraft would groan when the bay doors opened and then jerk when five or six tons suddenly dropped from its belly. Where would you want it dropped?"

"Right into the Atlantic Ocean without being detonated."

"Ohh, I see. I see. And then what happens?"

"When you reach the point where you were to drop the bomb, you tell bin Laden it's stuck. We'll arrange for the Yanks to scramble a few fighters to escort you down. They'll be arrested, and you go back to Pakistan. Guaranteed."

"How do you know you can trust me not to say anything?"

Malcolm smiled. "There's always cricket, old boy. But I've a less painful idea. I reckon Her Majesty's Government owes you several things. Would you accept a knighthood? Thought you might. But that's just a mere title, and I know you like money even more. Well, I have an idea. There's a Monet painting going up for auction at Sotheby's in a few weeks. Should fetch, oh, fifty million pounds. I can see you're interested in art."

"Oh, especially at that price."

"As I thought, dear boy. As a guarantee to us both, that we keep our bargain and you keep yours, we will buy it. I will get a code from Sotheby's. So shall you. It will identify either of us as the legitimate buyer. When you return from Washington, you get the Monet. All right, old chap?"

"A knighthood and a fifty-million-pound painting?"

"A Monet, dear boy, a Monet."

"Yes, yes. It's a deal, Mr. Malcolm."

After Khan left for his hotel—a four thousand dollar a night royal suite at Claridge's—Forbes-Smythe called in Tommy, Bob Cartwright, and Ayub el-Sahafat.

The Libyan bomb was now on British soil. Why not just replace it with a dummy? That way, they'd recoup a huge amount of investment and deprive Gaddafi of one of his bombs. The next step would be to get rid of bin Laden and Khan and their hangers-on. In so doing, rid the world of evil men and prevent every future evil deed. They'd have to pretend the bomb was real if Bob's idea was to work and be accepted by the government and the public when the "truth" finally emerged. The idea: blow up the plane in mid-air.

"Simple job. Conceal an explosive device to be detonated over water to avoid any irksome civilian casualties," Malcolm opined. "It could be detonated either by timer or satellite at the desired time."

"I think those lads at Brize Norton have seen enough of our BA 747," Bob said. "Any chance we can get it to leave from Heathrow? Surely Teddy can get one of his men with very big feet to plant the explosive, Malcolm?"

"He did well with that customs fuck-up even if the fuck-up was his own. Ayub, you're an expert with explosives. See any problems?"

"No. We just have to decide how to detonate it. I would suggest by satellite. That way we are covered if there are delays. We really don't want it going boom while sitting at the gate, do we, Malcolm?"

"Why, Ayub, I do believe you've been around us too long. You're beginning to sound like us. Not bad for a short Libyan infidel. Your Colonel won't be very happy about that."

"He'll be even less happy in a couple of days, Malcolm."

"Serves the bastard right. Lockerbie's revenge, I'd call it."

"Sir," Tommy asked, "how do we get British Airways to put on an extra flight to Washington? If this is to look kosher, the flight will have to be registered, have a gate, catered, and have flight crew apart from our special guests."

"Tommy, thank you for that very perceptive question. I have no fucking idea."

"Wait a minute," Bob interjected. "Suppose we say it's part of a top-secret diplomatic consignment on a Foreign Office charter. That should keep those snoopy-eyed customs bastards away. We'll present the proper papers and flight plans, of course. It'll be parked at a gate as usual, but only the tower and the British Airport Authority will know it's a special charter. Only they won't know how special."

"And how do we get Mr. bin Laden on board?" Malcolm asked Bob.

"We fly him from Libya into Brize Norton on our unmarked jet. We'll put everyone in BA uniforms, Khan included. They all simply arrive at the hangar in a BA bus and drive to Heathrow. Now, these fuckers *can* fly a 747, Ayub?"

"Yes," Ayub replied. "I've seen them in simulators and on the real things in Saudi. And if they keep their English to technical stuff, no one should notice any heavy accents. Remember, the Heathrow controllers hear pilots with accents all the time."

"From British Airways? Flying to Washington?" Forbes-Smythe asked.

"Ah, no."

"Can we arrange for it to take off at a very busy time, then?"

"It's always very busy, Malcolm," Ayub replied. "I wouldn't worry too much."

"And this from the genius who arranged the *Claudia* shipment."

Again, Ayub wanted to punch Forbes-Smythe in the head but knew far better. He had decided long ago that cricket was not his game.

***

Malcolm gave Teddy Williamson, the chief superintendent, the instructions Ayub had given him about the device. Williamson said he would do it personally.

Malcolm wondered about the sanity of that move and came up with a polite alternative. "Oh, aren't we silly here. Right here, in the Chief Petty Officer, we have the expert and the explosive. Teddy, can one of your folks get him to the plane? And then you won't have to be bothered having people wondering why you, of all people, is in the baggage hold of a BA 747."

"That's first-class thinking, Malcolm," Williamson replied. His sphincter had just dropped several notches.

"Ayub, okay by you?"

"If not, a full toss, is it, Malcolm?"

Williamson didn't know if this was a sexual or a cricket reference so pretended not to hear.

***

The unmarked private jet came to a halt at the far side of the airbase. Bob Cartwright sped around the airport perimeter in a British Airways crew bus and parked at the foot of the steps of the plane. The quite illegal passengers had already changed into their BA uniforms. Even A.K. Khan looked dashing in his epaulettes and jaunty pilot's cap. Two other sullen men and one woman silently climbed onto the bus. And then the tall gaunt figure of bin Laden, wearing an ignominious first officer's uniform, emerged. Tommy sat at the back with two armed Arabic-speaking agents as a precaution.

Bob turned the bus around and headed to the hangar. "How was the trip?" he asked bin Laden.

Although bin Laden understood and spoke English, he chose not to reply.

"Have it your way," Bob said, knowing that whatever words Mr. bin Laden said from now on would be among his last.

"The aircraft will be fully fuelled at Heathrow. Have we got a gate yet, Tommy?" Bob asked.

"We've got a gate and a flight number."

"Give them to me," one of the newly trained pilots demanded.

"You are British Airways flight zero niner eight. You use the word 'heavy' to denote that you are a jumbo jet."

"Do not tell me my job," the Arab snapped.

"Oh. Okay then. Your gate number is B sixteen. Air traffic control here at the base will give you your instructions and very quickly hand you over to Heathrow since we are so close. They will probably want you to fly north for a few minutes, gain some altitude, and when the air space is clear, bring you in. My two friends here will accompany you to Heathrow. Mr. Damian here speaks Arabic if you have any questions. Now call Brize Norton tower and get this thing rolling."

"Where is the bomb?" bin Laden asked in English.

"Hidden in this bay under the belly here. I can show you from inside," Khan said.

Bin Laden and Khan mounted the steps, entered the cold empty jumbo, and took an elevator down to the cargo hold. And there it was: snub-nosed and cradled in a steel sling-like apparatus, with wires and sensors projecting from it.

Khan thought the British had done a marvellous job making it look like the real bomb he had made in Libya.

What the British had not told Khan was that they had double-crossed him and he was staring at his own doomsday weapon.

***

Malcolm retreated to his ex-Temeraire with something nagging him. Nag. Nag. Nag. That one thing forced him to change his mind. He could not risk Khan finding a dummy bomb. The whole plot would collapse.

"But why? Why are the British allowing us to do this?" Ayub queried.

"I do not think they are. I think they or the Americans will try to shoot us down before we reach Washington. That way they get rid of the most-feared terrorist in the world and the world's greatest atomic bomb maker. But I have already outsmarted them. I have fitted my bomb with a Chinese M-11 booster rocket, and I will fire it a thousand miles sooner than anyone expects. Then we turn around, turn off all transponders and radios, and fly to Libya," Khan said.

"Will we have enough fuel?"

"Just."

"Brize Norton tower, this is BA heavy zero niner eight requesting permission to start engines."

"Permission granted, BA zero niner eight. Taxi to runway two six and hold."

"Roger."

Cartwright, el-Sahafat, and one of the agents climbed into the JIFFY van and headed back to Heathrow. They saw the 747 trundle down the runway and stop, awaiting take-off instructions.

"Holy fuck. I hope those crazy bastards are saying their prayers," Cartwright remarked.

On board, both bin Laden and Khan were deeply engrossed in the Qur'an, pretending not to be on a BA 747 flown by guys who had learned to fly in the Saudi desert and not in the spaghetti of flight paths over London.

The giant aircraft lurched forward slowly, very slowly gained speed, and miraculously lifted off the runway and howled its way to the north before receiving instructions to turn and float in on a glide path to Heathrow.

Detective Superintendent Teddy Williamson wasn't sure whether to shit bricks or shine his shoes when he saw the 747 with an atomic bomb on board lumber to a halt at gate B sixteen. Nothing had gone wrong! Nothing looked out of the ordinary. The tanker truck pumped fuel into the wings of the plane. The "captain" even did the usual walk-around to ensure everything was in order.

Williamson even felt a little lump in his throat as he took in the sight of two giant British Airways jumbo jets standing proudly side-by-side. The regular Washington flight had started boarding at gate B fifteen when the JIFFY bus pulled up outside his office.

He gave Ayub a pair of police overalls to wear and helped him load the explosive-laden backpack over his shoulders. He also slipped a police photo I.D. around "Constable Abdul Rahman's" neck, and then another uniformed officer and Ayub slid into a police van and dodged, wheeled, and weaved across the ant-ridden airport apron to the doomed 747.

To make it look real, baggage handlers were loading suitcases onto the plane. "Constable Rahman" handed his backpack to one of the handlers.

Ayub cringed and almost ducked when the handler tossed the backpack onto the conveyor belt. He watched it disappear with a *clunk* into the belly of the plane.

"All done, Ayub?" Forbes-Smythe inquired via a very secure telephone link to Heathrow.

"All done, Malcolm. What a morning! Bin Laden, those amateurs flying a 747, and then getting the explosive on board. Still, so far, so good, as you Brits would say. But I was surprised to see the 747 right beside our one."

"What do you mean?" Malcolm asked in a screeching whisper.

"Yes, there was the other scheduled BA 747 going to Washington."

"And it was parked beside ours?"

"Yes. I've got the gate numbers written down. B fifteen and B sixteen. But there's no problem. I had a cop with me to ensure things went okay."

"All right. Tommy, let's listen to Heathrow, shall we?"

"Heathrow ground control. BA charter heavy zero niner eight, please continue taxi to outer perimeter runway five niner left and hold for takeoff for Washington Dulles. Tower will take over."

"Roger BA zero niner eight, continuing to five niner left and hold for takeoff to Washington Dulles. Will wait on Heathrow tower. Thank you, ground control."

"BA heavy zero niner eight, Heathrow tower. You will be followed on the same flight path by BA heavy two one seven. Separation will be twenty, I repeat, twenty miles."

"Roger."

"BA heavy zero niner eight, you are cleared for takeoff."

"Roger. Zero niner eight cleared for takeoff. Good afternoon, sir."

"Don't fucking overdo it," a worried Malcolm said.

"Ground control to BA heavy two one seven."

"Two one seven."

"Your slot closes in three minutes. What is your status?"

"BA two one seven is closing all doors now and ready for pushback."

"Roger, two one seven."

The scheduled passenger flight had 280 passengers on board that day. A couple of senators in first class. Two television executives and their wives. In the back, a girls basketball team. And the usual detritus of the tired and the excited travellers, who haunt the universe twenty-four hours a day.

"BA two one seven, you are cleared for takeoff. Please report in at the outer marker and turn two seven zero."

"Roger."

The pitch of the engines droned and then sputtered into a scream as the heavily laden jumbo lurched clumsily down the runway and lifted gracefully into the air with a trail of kerosene spewing from its four massive engines.

"We should give them an hour to clear the coast. Then we'll blow the fuckers out of the sky and it's goodbye bin Laden, goodbye Khan, and hello Monet, only you didn't hear that last bit." Malcolm was almost giggly at the prospect.

The Prime Minister and Cabinet had approved the plan. The military were on side. Even Her Majesty, who conceded that although the loss of any human life was horrid, had made an exception in this case.

Malcolm Forbes-Smythe was recalling every detail of that royal morning briefing, still obsessed, still trying to find any flaws. He had accompanied the Prime Minister to Buckingham Palace for a special morning tea.

As the Queen had slathered her morning scones with Marmite, a habit she'd acquired in one of her colonies, she remarked: "Oh, that place where the darkies poked their tongues out at me and what's his name, my husband, um, Philip the Grecian, rubbed his nose with theirs, all perfectly horrid, and they played this silly game called rugby, well, it's just not cricket, is it?"

"No, ma'am," an obsequious John Major had responded.

Will this silly old bitch ever get to the point, Malcolm wondered.

"I mean to say. Mmm. This is rather splendid. Are you sure you won't have any? Not the Marmite. That's for me. But you may have a scone and a small pat of butter, should you desire it."

Both men demurred, especially when one of the royal Corgis crapped on the carpet, the smell of which even overpowered the Marmite.

"Oh, I say, what a naughty boy. No, not you, Mr. Major. My little doggie. He's done do-dos on your shoe as well as the carpet. No, don't touch it. A prime minister should not have to clean up after one of my doggies does do-dos on his shoes. I'll ring for a footman. I say, a footman to clean his shoes. That's rather jolly, don't you think?"

John Major was thinking he would like to kick the fucking mongrel through the palace windows and have a fucking double-decker bus flatten the little shitter.

"Now, about your precious bomb. Oh, footman, the Prime Minister has some do-dos on his shoes. Would you remove it, please?"

"Wot is 'shoo'?"

"No, you philistine. The do-dos."

"Beg your pardon, Your Most Majestyful Majesty, but I ain't touchin' that with a ten-foot tiara."

"There's no such thing as a ten-foot tiara, you stupid little man."

"My bruvvers in the union would not like to hear wot it was you asked me to do, Your Most Gracious Majesty, ma'am."

"Oh, those silly unions. Equal pay and all that rubbish. Sorry, Mr. Major, but would you mind running off to the wee boys' room and clean that nasty mess off your shoes? Oh, and give the carpet a bit of a rub while you're down there."

"Of course, Your Majesty," he replied happily though his teeth were clenched so tightly his jaw was about to break.

"So Mr. Forbes-Smythe… Oh, I say, that is a nice bright blue tie. But, of course, you are a homosexual so you know about colours and things of that nature. I say, you could even help me with my azaleas."

"Well, it takes a queen to know a queen," Forbes-Smythe replied.

"Oh, I say, that's going a bit jolly far, Mr. Forbes-Smythe. But it is rather naughty. Now, there's something I've wondered about homosexuals for many years. Philip says he's never tried it. Do they actually insert their... Their—well, you know..."

"Penis?"

"Mr. Forbes-Smythe! How dare you use that word in front of me."

"What word was that?" the returning John Major, devoid of shit and derision, asked.

"Penis," Forbes-Smythe replied.

"Penis?" Major asked.

"Penis," Forbes-Smythe said.

"Gentlemen, that is enough! I merely wanted to know if homosexuals inserted their petunias in seedling boxes in spring, or did they get a better bloom by waiting a few weeks? I won't hear any talk about penises. I say, is that the correct plural? Or should it be 'peni'?"

"Why, how many do you want?" Malcolm enquired.

"I don't want any! But that tart Diana would know the plural of penis. My word, yes. That common little whore is penis-crazy. I'm told she likes them big and throbbing and hard as rocks and loves to slip her moist mouth... I say, got off track a bit there. Now, about your bomb."

"My what?" Major asked.

"Your bomb. Your bomb."

"Oh. Oh, ha, ha, I thought you said my bum. Ha, ha."

"Of course I wasn't enquiring as to the welfare of your bum. I don't care about it one whit, Mr. Major, is that clear? Now about this atomic bum—I mean bomb—would it go off in the explosion?"

"No, ma'am." John Major explained that it had to be detonated separately. However, a fleet of Royal Navy ships, submarines, and the two carriers *Illustrious* and *Ark Royal* were at sea, waiting to direct operations to recover the bomb. The carriers also had full squadrons of fighter-bombers on board should they be required.

"Why on earth should we require fighter bombers, Mr. Major?"

"Just in case something goes wrong."

Fifty-five minutes had gone by since the bomb-carrying jumbo left Heathrow. It had cleared Ireland and was heading out over the Atlantic. Communications with the aircraft had dropped to a minor course alteration here, a slight altitude change there.

On board, bin Laden sat in economy class as a matter of principle and continued to read the Qur'an. Khan, up in first class, toyed with his remote control that was meant to send the bomb on its way. The two pilots seemed relaxed, even enjoying the ride. The lone woman had changed out of her uniform and was now veiled. She also carried an AK-47, but Khan was too preoccupied to wonder why. The Bravo Alpha zero niner eight had reached its cruising altitude and was on course to deliver a cataclysm.

"Blow it now, Malcolm?" Ayub asked.

"Now."

Ayub picked up the phone. "This is control. Operation Lockerbie Revenge. Code one-six-one-two-one-one-two-two-two-one-one-two-two. Confirm, please. Thank you. Initiate action now."

They listened intently to the intercom still patched through from Heathrow. It would take about a second and a half for the signal to reach the satellite that, in turn, would detonate the bomb and blow zero niner eight into the Atlantic Ocean and end the terror wreaked by bin Laden and Khan.

"Get Heathrow to call them up. Confirm they don't answer. I can't stand the bloody silence," Malcolm ordered Tommy.

"London Heathrow calling Bravo Alpha zero niner eight. Bravo Alpha zero niner eight, do you copy?"

"Roger Heathrow, Bravo Alpha zero niner eight. Do you have another change for us?"

"Wait one."

"Roger."

Malcolm stared at Bob. "They're still in the air. What the fuck has happened? Didn't the bomb go off?"

"Malcolm! Malcolm! Listen."

"Heathrow Tower calling Bravo Alpha two one seven. Two one seven. We have lost you from radar. Reply please, two one seven. Supervisor! We've lost BA two one seven to Washington. It's just disappeared from my radar, sir."

"Jesus Christ," Malcolm screamed. "We've blown up the wrong fucking plane! Ayub, you stupid, stupid bastard!

You put the bomb in the wrong fucking plane! The wrong fucking plane. We've just killed three hundred people! And the other one is headed for Washington with a real atomic bomb on board. Oh, Jesus! Tommy, get the PM. Now!"

Already Malcolm could see the TV screen in his office carrying newsflashes about the plane lost from radar.

Neither Prime Minister John Major nor Malcolm Forbes-Smythe was in the most effervescent of moods.

"I know, John, I know. But, first, we've got to stop that plane with the bomb. No, it's real. John, John, calm down. Well, let's talk about that when this is over. Those aircraft carriers. They've got fully armed jets on board. Harriers, yes, I know. John, we'll have to scramble a dozen of them to chase the 747 and shoot it down. Yes, you'll have to give the order. I suggest we don't waste another second, John, or it'll be out of the Harriers' range."

On the 747, the two pilots heard the Heathrow exchange and switched to Arabic.

"That was meant to be us! They were going to blow us up, not shoot us down!"

"Oh, no! Someone's going to have to tell the sleeping scarecrow in economy. That'll be me. And I always wanted to be the captain of a 747!"

"Osama. Osama, wake up! The British have blown up the other plane going to Washington. It's a mistake, I'm sure. They were going to blow us up!"

Bin Laden sprang to his feet, arms, legs, and every other appendage he could muster. He didn't see the voluptuous venality of virgins he'd been promised. Bin Laden saw death. And death screamed its black cloak almost off its mortal toil.

"Khan! When can you fire the atomic bomb? I want it to destroy London. Will it reach London from here?" The scythe of death slashed ever closer as Osama went, as it were, ballistic.

Khan didn't care when he fired it because he still thought it was a dummy. "Let me do some calculations."

"Quickly. The British will be sending up planes to shoot us down. We must calibrate the bomb before that and try to outrun them to Libya. Khan, do you have the calculations yet?"

"I do, Osama. If we turn now and maintain this airspeed, I can fire the missile in exactly six minutes, and it will explode directly over Central London. I estimate it will kill one million people immediately and destroy almost the entire city."

Khan's calculations were real. He loved this game, even if a fantasy.

"Turn the plane," bin Laden softly ordered the pilots.

"How many minutes left, Khan?" bin Laden asked.

"Three, Osama. In three minutes, beautiful London will resemble Hiroshima. It's basically the same bomb, only better."

"Good. Good. Allah, may peace be upon Him, will reward us richly. Allahu Akbar."

They all repeated the call.

"Allahu Akbar."

"Ninety seconds, Osama."

The first Hawker Sea Harrier catapulted up the specially bent high bow of the aircraft carrier fully loaded with air-to-air missiles and canons. Two more followed. Their top speed was 750 miles an hour, two hundred miles per hour faster than a 747. But without added fuel tanks, they had a dismal range of only 230 miles.

On the bridge of the *Ark Royal*, the commander saw the jumbo turn back towards him. "What's the silly bugger doing?"

Malcolm knew exactly what he was doing. "Jesus. He's going to drop it over London! How long before the Harriers reach it?"

"The carrier says the latest ETA is one minute and twenty seconds." Tommy was handling three phones and two intercoms.

Ayub knew he had to get out. These bastards would kill him the moment they got a chance. At the moment, they were so fixated on the bomb on the plane they wouldn't notice anything else. He knew he would take the fall. He'd be branded as a spy who deliberately put the explosive on the wrong plane. Another Libyan act of terrorism. Gaddafi would execute him this time. He had to get out. Now! And even if he didn't, there was a chance he'd be incinerated by the bomb he helped create.

"One minute to bomb launch," Khan announced convincingly.

Bin Laden stared at the control in the Pakistani's hands and said a prayer, praising Allah. In one minute, the capital city of Great Britain, with its huge Christian churches and despicable royal family and the class system, would be in ashes and generations would praise Allah, may peace be upon Him.

"Thirty seconds, Malcolm."

Suddenly, Cartwright lunged at Ayub, who'd pulled out a gun. He squeezed his carotid artery so hard that the Chief Petty Officer was dead within seconds.

"There! There is it," the lead Harrier pilot radioed. "I can get it in about five seconds."

"Fire when ready."

"What was that?" Bin laden looked up. What he saw was mystifying and horrific.

The two pilots were slumped over the controls. Blood trickled from small holes in the backs of their heads.

"Fire! Fire! Fire!" he screamed at Khan in English.

A moment later, a bullet exploded Khan's head.

The woman in the covered veil was Bob Cartwright's contribution. She was Marie Khatab, CIA. Without hesitating, she tore bin Laden to pieces with her AK-47. She had to take the chance that the bullets wouldn't pierce the fuselage.

"I've got it now," the Harrier pilot radioed. "Preparing to fire."

Security guard Ali Khab raced to the front of the plane and picked up the radio. "Don't sh—"

Two missiles hit BA 098. It blew apart at thirty-five thousand feet and crashed into the churning Atlantic.

***

"Yes, Prime Minister. Of course, Prime Minister. I understand there will have to be statements of condolence from both you and the Queen. But if I may, John, I think there is something we can do. No, Prime Minister, please listen. Every al-Qaeda member in the world thinks bin Laden is dead and that we killed him. For sure, they'll be planning a major operation to retaliate. I don't know, but it will be big. But what if he's not dead? Hello? John? Oh, I thought I had lost you. No, John, I assure you my marbles and other appendages are where they should be. The only people who knew he was actually on that plane are either dead or sworn under the Official Secrets Act. And that's only a couple of your people and mine, anyhow. You know that actor we use occasionally to issue al-Qaeda statements? Yes, him. By the way, do you remember when the CIA swore he was speaking from the Afghan border? Their experts could tell from the texture of the rock behind him? Yes, but it was actually an old wall near the Ealing picture studios. Well, why don't we get him to dress up as bin Laden? Have the makeup boys—yes, boys—John, turn him into the sheik. And we'll put him on the al-Qaeda website. Oh, he'll condemn us, say Allah was with him and that he is safe and declare another all-out warfare, etc., etc., but we'd better do it soon before they actually do start blowing up London or Paris or Washington. No, John. This won't be a cock-up. Remember, the Chief Petty Officer was a double agent and he, in reality, blew both planes up. And he tried to kill me. Oh, by the way, are you going to Islamabad for A.K.'s service. After all, he was a Pakistani hero. Hello? Hello?"

CHAPTER TWENTY-THREE

Brian Hendricks was an Anglo-Indian, about six feet five, with a light lilting voice that spoke perfect Arabic, regional accents and all. He didn't do much acting work apart from strange calls from Whitehall. Still, they paid him a hundred pounds an hour and all he had to do was imitate some Arab or another darker-skinned person, say some outrageous rubbish, sign the Official Secrets Act, and bugger off to the pub.

The JIFFY van found him walking back to his Paddington flat after a pint of Red Barrel and a steak and kidney pie at his local.

"In you get, lad," the agent ordered as they pulled alongside.

"Who are you?"

"Whitehall's got a job for you."

"Oh, why didn't you say? Can I dash home and clean up a bit?"

"Not today, lad. This one's a rush job."

"Hasn't got anything to do with those planes crashing, has it?"

"Don't know, lad. Even if I did, wouldn't tell you."

***

Malcolm's office now resembled a dressing room behind The London Palladium, London's massive concert hall.

"Who's he to be today, Malcolm?" Joey, one of the three make-up artists, asked.

"Osama bin Laden."

"But isn't he dead, Malcolm?"

"That depends on how good you are, Joey."

"And wardrobe, Malcolm?"

"She'll be here in a minute. Just picking up Mr. bin Laden's outfit from Finsbury Market."

At that moment, the agent entered the room with Brian Hendricks.

"Oh, Brian, thank you for coming. This will take about four hours, but if you do a bang-up job, we'll make it an even five hundred cash. How does that sound?"

"Rather good, Mr. Forbes-Smythe. Do you have a TV recording of this man? I've done him before, as you know, but I want to make sure I get the gestures and the voice exactly right."

"Tommy, take Brian into the communications room and let him do the translation, get the voice thing right. Joey, you and your rather pretty friends will have to carry on in there, too."

"Carry on, Malcolm? You coming, too?"

"Now, Joey, don't be cheeky. When Brian comes back, I want to see Osama, got it?"

"All right, dear. But where will you film this epic?"

"Just to piss the CIA off, we'll do it right here in my office, but he'll have a plain grey sheet behind him. It'll drive them crazy trying to figure out where he is. We'll deliberately distort the sound a bit and shoot it on a very cheap camera. By the time we hack it onto the al-Qaeda site, he'll be the real thing. Very alive but still quite dead."

Cartwright went ashen for a second, and then came to his senses. "Jesus, you guys have done a great job. I really thought it was bin Laden."

"Okay, Brian, read it a few more times, and then we'll do a take."

Tommy thought the lighting was too professional, so they turned off all the lights in the office except for one for "Osama" to read by. They then decided to shoot it without any lights. That way, it would look really shitty, like a true al-Qaeda video.

"Ah, excuse me, Mr. Forbes-Smythe," Brian politely asked, "would bin Laden use the phrase 'and for all mankind'?"

"No. You're right, Brian. Change it to 'for all the followers of Allah, may peace be upon Him.' Anything else glaring, Brian?"

"No. This looks like a speech he would deliver. I'm ready if you are."

Tommy rolled the camera, with the tripod slightly askew, and Brian was on. His head bowed in prayer for about fifteen seconds, and then he raised it and gazed into the lens. He spoke in bin-Laden's soft Saudi-accented Arabic, which was monitored by the Arabic-speaking agent Damian Walpole, who'd been on the British Airways bus at Brize Norton. "Bin Laden's" speech would be sub-titled in not-too-perfect English.

"Allah, may peace be upon Him, spared me today. In His glory and wisdom, He prevented me from getting on that death machine. In his wisdom, Allah, praise be His holy name, He took two martyrs. He also took a brother in Islam and one infidel. The foolish British and Americans will never defeat the forces of our great Allah, may peace be upon Him. I call on all jihadists to bring down a giant wave of violent death upon all infidels. I call on all jihadists to follow Allah, may peace be upon Him, and to follow me to the great victory that will soon be ours. Allahu Akbar. Allahu Akbar. God is great. God is great."

"Nice job, Brian. Well done."

Brian frowned, obviously puzzled. "So he's really dead, is he?"

"No, Brian, you just brought him back to life. Ever thought of going into the Jesus business?"

***

AL-QAEDA STUNNER. BIN LADEN ALIVE. The news was almost bigger than the two jumbo jets. Everyone bought it.

The CIA said they needed to do further analysis, but all indications were that the tape was genuine, the voice had been scientifically authenticated, and their experts were of the opinion that the sheet was typical of the kind used by the upper classes in the Khat district of Afghanistan. Bin Laden himself looked a little older than when last seen on the internet, and the pallor of his skin indicated he still suffered from kidney trouble.

Malcolm may have lost the IRA, but he had just gained al-Qaeda.

"Talking of those clowns at the CIA, Malcolm, I think you can now call off the search for the A-bomb," Bob Cartwright opined from his pretentious nautical chair opposite Malcolm at the Vauxhall Bridge HQ of MI6.

"But it's only been a week. Plus they're still finding remains from the Washington flight."

"They might as well keep doing that, but the bomb's a waste of time."

"What do you mean?"

"Malcolm, old buddy, you're not gonna like this, but that bomb at the bottom of the Atlantic is a dummy. A fake."

"What the fuck are you talking about, Bob?" Malcolm's vocal range shot miraculously into the range of a countertenor, sirening to two octaves above middle C—or G above that.

Bob enjoyed the moonlight serenade so much he gave Malcolm an extended encore. "Malcolm, I'm still an American, and I just could not risk those evil bastards getting through despite all the precautions, so one night I had my boys take the real bomb to a secure place and put in the dummy."

"But people died and—"

"That was your fuck-up, old buddy. You trusted that fucking Libyan to do your dirty work, and remember, I lost a good agent on that plane your Navy shot down. I put her there for you, Malcolm."

"I know. I know, Bob. But... Jesus! You should have told me."

"Couldn't do it, old buddy. Me. I trust only myself."

But there were still several bright spots in Malcolm's life. John Major believed that Ayub was a spy and had wrecked the entire operation, so Malcolm wasn't fired.

And the PM loved the bin Laden scam. "Genius, dear boy. Genius."

The British and U.S. navies poured April showers of missiles into Gaddafi's hidden nuclear facilities and did, indeed, scatter them to the four corners of his very real desert.

Khan got a hero's funeral in Pakistan, but he didn't get the Monet!

CHAPTER TWENTY-FOUR

He rarely did it, but a chipper Forbes-Smythe stepped out into the dull afternoon and flagged down a taxi. All by himself.

"Where to, guv?"

"Sotheby's, please."

"New Bond Street, right, guv?"

"Right."

Twenty minutes later, Malcolm entered a world in which he felt he truly belonged. High art, obscene prices, and a flotilla of gay attendants.

"Welcome, sir. It's Mr. Forbes-Smythe, correct? Or should I say what the grapevine's saying about you: Sir Malcolm Forbes-Smythe?"

"Oh, don't believe the grapevine unless it's very well-hung with luscious fruit, if you know what I mean."

"Quite so, sir. How very true. Now, how can I help you? I know. I'm so sorry, sir. It's about the Monet. Am I right, sir?"

"The Monet, yes."

"I must say it was extraordinarily generous of you, sir. Very generous, indeed."

"What are you talking about?"

"Oh, come on, sir, you don't have to be modest with me. We all thought you did a marvellous thing."

"Fucking Khan!"

"I BEG your pardon, sir! I cannot have that language in this emporium."

"I said 'Khan'! Khan! As in Khan, the A-bomb master."

"Oh, I see. I misunderstood. Forgive me, sir. No, but that wasn't the gentleman's name."

"It wasn't?"

"No, sir. It was the gentleman of the Arabic press, Mr. Mustaffa Fakih."

"Fucking Fakih!"

"Now, sir, I warned you about the language!"

"No, you bloody idiot. Fakih, the newspaperman. How did he get involved?"

"He came in with that special code that you said only two people in the world had and that I was to give the Monet to either of you."

Forbes-Smythe's stomach lurched, just as it had when he'd heard those Arabs come back on the intercom. "And what did this Mr. Fakih say?"

"That over the last few years he had made friends with a gentleman from Pakistan."

"Fucking Khan!"

"I won't warn you again, sir. You must stop using such language here."

Malcolm had seen carotid squeezes often enough and reckoned he could kill this little poofter at that very moment.

"Tell me about the painting!" He was almost yelling.

"It seems this Pakistani gentleman was going on a trip, but he wanted Mr. Fakih to pick up the Monet and deliver to a place of your choosing."

Malcolm brightened considerably. "Here in London?"

"Oh, no, sir. Mr. Fakih said that his friend told him you would like to donate the painting to a very old gallery that had been badly damaged and that you would like to help them rebuild their collection, starting with the Monet. Indeed, he said you were a personal friend of the President, who would take very good care of it."

"But I've never met the President of the United States."

"The United States? Oh, that's a good one, sir. Very droll. No, we shipped it off under armed guard just last week."

"And where, may I ask, did you ship it?"

"Just as you requested, sir, to Libya."

"Libya! To fucking Colonel Muammar fucking Gaddafi! You fucking great berk! He blew up the Lockerbie jet and those two over the Atlantic. He's armed the IRA and the PLO and has killed hundreds of people. It was a double-cross! Khan made an atomic bomb for him! And was getting even with me for a game of cricket! Now Gaddafi's got the Monet! My Monet. And I'll never get it back!"

"Oh, dear me. What a terrible day for you, sir. But I've got just the thing to cheer you up. A game of cricket, sir?"

SONG CREDITS

“Giant Steps” - John Coltrane (1926-1967)

“If I Give Up the Saxophone Will You Come Back to Me?” - Eddie Cantor (1892-1964)

“It Must Be Jelly Coz Jam Don’t Shake Like That” - Louis Jordan (1908-1975)

“I’ve Got a Lovely Bunch of Coconuts” - Fred Heatherton (comp.1944)

“Peanut Vendor” Trad. Cuban - *“El Manisero”*

“Salt Peanuts” - Dizzy Gillespie (1917-1973)

“Spinning Wheel” - Blood, Sweat and Tears (1967-1985)

“Swanee” - George Gershwin (1909-1937)

ABOUT THE AUTHOR

John Scully is an international award-winning Canadian journalist who has produced news stories, investigative reports, and documentaries in over seventy countries.

He has worked for world leaders in journalism, such as BBC TV News and *Current Affairs*; Canadian Television (CTV), including *W5* and the CTV National News; and the Canadian Broadcasting Corporation, including the *National,* the *Journal,* and the *5th Estate*.

He was also Head of Current Affairs at TVNZ (Television New Zealand). He has trained senior journalists across Canada and around the world.

Scully has survived thirty-six war zones. He has covered stories and investigations in all the countries mentioned in this, his new book *A Comedy of Terror*, except for Afghanistan and North Korea.

He has published two previous books: *Am I Dead Yet?* and *Am I Sane Yet*?

Scully lives in Toronto, Ontario, Canada, with his wife, two adult children, and one grandson.

Reviews (good or bad) are important to authors.
Please leave a review wherever possible.

Manufactured by Amazon.ca
Bolton, ON

25654128R00116